THE SPIDER:
THE COMING OF THE TERROR

THE SPIDER

MASTER OF MEN!

THE COMING OF
THE TERROR

By Grant Stockbridge

STEEGER BOOKS • 2020

CHAPTER 1
STRIPPED OF WEALTH

PROBABLY NO criminal whom Richard Wentworth ever fought for the liberty and safety of mankind earned at once so much of his hatred—yet so much of his respect—as the man who ruined him. The man who came out of the East and struck with such shrewd, swift energy, with such incredibly keen foresight that within a few hours of his first brutal blow, Wentworth was stripped of wealth and power—was fleeing, a hunted criminal, through the streets of his beloved city!

It seems incredible, but thanks to the diaries which Wentworth's brave love, Nita van Sloan, kept so faithfully, there can be no question of its truth. At one o'clock that afternoon, Wentworth was laughing gaily in a mock-combat of sabers on the terrace of his penthouse; yet an hour afterward....

Wentworth himself could not understand the thing which happened there on the terrace beneath the heat of the August sunlight. He was stripped to bathing trunks, canvas shoes on his feet, and his man, Jackson, was similarly dressed. The sun glittered on the swift steel of their sabers. They wore no masks, no plastrons or gauntlets. For a while this assault was a game, Wentworth's knowledge of swordsmanship was not mere sport. More times than he could remember, his life, the lives of hundreds, had hung on the skill and strength of his sword-wrist!

The sun was hot. His lean, tanned, body glistened with

The march of conquest had begun.

perspiration, his muscles rippled smoothly flat under healthy skin. Jackson was pressing him hard, his Gascon face grim. Joy mounted within Wentworth, pumped jubilantly through his veins—and then, for no reason at all, he felt cold. The coldness touched his spine near its base, crept up toward his brain and spread tingling out over his shoulders, along his arms. And Jackson's questing point almost found his breast!

With a quick beat, Wentworth drove the saber aside. He struck twice, three times, with lightning-swift swirls of the

blade, then abruptly thrust. His remarkable control stopped the steel just as its tip pricked Jackson's left breast and his man stepped back, saluted and smiled. The fighting fury that had been upon him lingered in the tightness about his lips. But Wentworth did not seem to see. He stood frowning out into the sunlight glare, sword point resting on his toe, face lifting as if he quested for something unseen and unseeable, but still there all about him.

From the shadows, a gaunt-framed man in the white robes and turban of the East slipped forward on bare, silent feet and laid a flannel robe across Wentworth's shoulders. Absently, Wentworth handed the saber to the man, a Sikh by his curling full beard. The Hindu took the sword reverently, as becomes a fighting man, and Wentworth walked away from the two faithful ones who served him, moved to the parapet and gazed out over the buildings of his beloved city toward the blue sparkle of New York harbor. There was a sleek liner making its slowing way up the river to dock and, gazing at it, Wentworth knew once more that touch of cold to his spine.

Jackson and the Sikh, Ram Singh, gazed at each other, then both swung to look at Wentworth. Without a word, the two men drew together and Jackson slowly pulled on a robe. His hand dropped to a pocket and, deliberately, he checked over the automatic pistol that rested there. The master they served was never wholly free from danger and when, as now, he went into abstraction in the midst of joyous excitement....

"*Wah!*" whispered Ram Singh, "there is a mighty battle before us, my comrade!"

Jackson said nothing, but the heavy muscles of his jaws swelled and tightened. He nodded gravely.

"Wah!" intoned Ram Singh again. His hand strayed to the hilt of the knife at his sash girdle. There was a fierce gleam in his dark eyes.

This was at a little after one o'clock and the Man from the East had not yet landed in New York, though he had set his murderers to work before him. He was on that ship at which Wentworth gazed. These are not things that can be readily explained, but the diaries that Nita van Sloan kept do not lie. And within the next hour, the hell that would yawn for Richard Wentworth and all the city he held dear would begin to open it gates!

WENTWORTH WHIRLED from the railing and, striding toward his men, knotted his robe about him.

"Ram Singh," he spoke crisply, "go to the bank vault and bring me twenty thousand—no, fifty thousand dollars. If there is not that much cash, bring government bonds."

Ram Singh swept a salaam, cupped hands to his forehead. *"Han, sahib!"* he breathed. "It is a command!" He pivoted and started away, but Wentworth called him back. He laid a hand on the Sikh's shoulder and his gray-blue eyes lost their abstraction and held a kindly light.

"Thy eyes, warrior," he said gently, "they are keen again?"

Ram Singh's teeth glittered amid his black beard. He lifted his eyes to the sky and there in the heavens hung a black speck.

"That, master," he said, "is an Army Boeing attack ship."

Wentworth peered up where he pointed, studied the speck for a moment, caught up binoculars from a near-by table, and focused them. He smiled then. "Thy eyes are better than ever, thou eagle," he said. His face grew grim. "I have had a warning, Ram Singh! I know not its origin or cause. Use thy eyes, Ram Singh! Use them well!"

Ram Singh's head lifted proudly and his hand touched his knife hilt. With another low salaam he stalked away. Wentworth watched him go, still frowning a little. The gallant Sikh had been blinded in his service by a pernicious vapor loosed by criminals. It was only after long

ISIS

months that his sight had been restored. And now they must plunge into another maelstrom of battle and crime. Wentworth knew that, without question, for he was too wise not to heed the promptings of his subconscious.

"Jackson," he said abruptly, "the *Brittanic* is coming up the North River. I want its passenger list."

Jackson saluted, heeled about and marched off.

It was madness, Wentworth counseled himself, to pay such heed to this sudden premonition. Because of no more than that, he was withdrawing a large sum of money from the vaults where he kept ready cash; he was keyed to a high tension.... He jerked his head, strode toward his penthouse, a man just under six feet, hard bones packed with lithe muscle, with a swing to his shoulders at once athletic and confident, and the poise of his head— kings might have striven for just that commanding carriage, that subtly arrogant strength, but few would have attained its perfection. There was nothing studied about Wentworth's bearing. He was a man's man, born to command.

It was, as Wentworth walked into his penthouse, precisely a quarter of two….

He bathed swiftly, donned a suit of dark tropical worsted, strode with his long, determined pace back to the drawing room and forced himself to remain rooted in one position. His lean fingers were without a tremor as he drew a cigarette from a slim platinum case and lighted it. But, abruptly, he hurled the scarcely touched cigarette into the fireplace, strode into the hallway where there was a telephone.

When the switchboard operator answered from the hallway on the first floor, Wentworth said shortly, "Close guard!"

For a moment he felt vaguely ridiculous. For no real reason he had closed the armed guard he kept always within the building. He owned the entire structure crowned by his duplex penthouse, had bought it as a precaution of safety. He dropped the phone into its cradle, strode toward his room where he had a private line. As he reached for the instrument, its bell pealed and he lifted it with a swift up-rush of eagerness. This wire went directly to the apartment of his fiancée, the one woman in the world who shared his travails, who knew his secrets….

"Hello, Nita," he cried. He thrust aside his trepidations, rushed on gaily. "How perfectly is thy mystic *karma* attuned to mine! Even now I hastened to call thee…."

Nita laughed softly, but there was a dubious, uncertain note in her voice. "I'm glad to find you so cheerful, Dick. Somehow, I have a feeling…."

"Well, what?" Wentworth's voice rasped abruptly.

"Ah!" Nita cried. "Then you have felt it, too? There is something threatening, Dick, something I can feel like a storm in the air. Are you on guard, Dick lover?"

THE CRY that came feebly to Wentworth's ears whipped him from the phone, took his eyes to the doorway of his room. He said steadily into the phone, "I'll call you later, dear."

He hung up, as the cry came again.

Wentworth's heart gave a frantic leap. In a long bound, he reached the doorway, pivoted into the hall. As he raced toward the service entrance of the apartment whence the cry came, his right hand crossed his chest and thereafter he ran with a heavy automatic pistol in his fist.

For he had recognized that cry. His keen ears had detected the distress, the failing strength, of Ram Singh! He reached the service door, whipped it open and went out, gun first. On the tiled floor lay the crumpled body of the powerful Sikh! His white clothing was torn and stained with great streaks of his own blood.

The shout that tore from Wentworth's own lips and went clapping through the empty hallway was a fierce challenge. He sprang toward the stairway, the elevator that led downward—and stopped. He stood, rigidly, listening, waiting, his gun questing like a hound's nose that tests the wind. He sprang back to the door then, pressed a button, and knew that throughout the building alarm fights and buzzers were flashing his warning: "Close the building. Let no one leave!"

He lifted Ram Singh with a single heave of his powerful arms,

carried him like a baby through the
penthouse hallway to the man's own
room and stretched him on the bed.
Swiftly he ripped free the remnants
of the clothing. Jackson came to the
doorway while he worked, and over
his shoulder Wentworth flung swift

orders to search for Ram Singh's assailant. But Jackson was not
to leave the penthouse! And the order now was: "Close siege!"

All his premonitions came to a head in this single swift blow.
For no reason at all, Wentworth looked at the watch upon his
wrist. It was one minute after two o'clock....

His preliminary examination indicated that except for a swelling lump on his skull, Ram Singh was not seriously wounded.
His knife was gone, the great knife that he never drew save to
kill. Wentworth made a swift calculation and shook his head.
Ram Singh had had ample time to reach the bank and return....

As he gazed down upon Ram Singh, the Sikh started up
wildly. He stared up into his master's eyes for a moment, then
flung himself to the floor on his knees.

"Master!" he cried. "Master, I have failed thee!"

Wentworth smiled, shook his head. "Come, warrior, for thy
kind there can be no failure. A defeat perhaps, but there will be
a vengeance!"

Ram Singh swayed his head in woeful grief. "Master, master,
you do not know! When thy servant reached the vault, he
received thy further order to take everything from the vault...."

A start jerked at Wentworth's muscles. He scarcely restrained it and his hands reached quickly for the Sikh's shoulders, his fingers bit deep. "All in the vault, Ram Singh?" he asked softly.

"*Han, sahib!* Everything!" Wentworth shook his head, stepped back a pace. He was a wealthy man, but that vault had held a great proportion of his ready cash; more than a half million in bills and easily negotiable bonds!

"Go on!" he said harshly. "I gave no such order!" His harshness was not for Ram Singh—it was the tension in his breast.

"Thy servant obeyed, master," Ram Singh said humbly. "With everything from the vault, thy servant went to the street. There was a man of the police beside the car. He declared thy servant had parked improperly, though this was not so. While we argued, one struck thy servant suddenly from behind. One of them, *sahib*, the knife slew! They were blackamoors, *sahib*, who attacked thy servant. The blow had injured his sight again and, presently when they were gone, thy wealth was gone also. They had vanished… *Slay thy servant, master, for he has failed thee!*"

Wentworth stood staring at the wall. Coming on the heels of his premonition of peril—it had been no more than that—this robbery was ominous. It was even more. It was clear that he was under close surveillance, that someone had known enough of his habits, his routine, to be able to leave a message at the bank which would make certain that Ram Singh carried the entire contents of his safe deposit boxes when be left the bank. A false policeman had been planted to hold Ram Singh's attention. And Negroes—to Ram Singh they would be blackamoors—had committed the actual robbery!

WENTWORTH'S KEEN eyes narrowed. It seemed,

almost, that someone might have been watching him so closely that they had learned his most closely guarded secret! There was a figure of the night, terrible to those who were outside the law, known throughout the Underworlds of the earth as the Spider. This man who carried a terrible vengeance to those who sinned against humanity, this Spider, was hunted on a hundred charges by the police. That his crimes were always committed to punish miscreants, to protect the people, did not matter. And this Nemesis of the evil, the strange secret figure was in truth— Richard Wentworth!

But no one knew that, no one could know it who would betray him. Nita van Sloan, Jackson, Ram Singh—these knew it, but any of them would have died before revealing the fact. Yet, this strange power which had struck at him had apparently penetrated one of the unvarying customs of the Spider! When battle threatened, Wentworth invariably converted large sums of securities into cash. For money was a potent weapon in any battle against the Underworld....

A violent oath rasped in Wentworth's throat. "They planned well!" he said harshly. "Let not my warrior... *Stop, Ram Singh!*"

While Wentworth had sunk into abstraction, he had forgotten the abject misery of the Sikh. Now, he saw that Ram Singh had snatched up his automatic from the table, that already he had pressed the muzzle to his breast. In Ram Singh's code, a servant failed his master only once; the reasons for that failure could not matter. And Ram Singh was a warrior, of a tribe of kings. His service of Wentworth was the voluntary tribute of one strong man to another—He had failed the man he worshiped with a fierceness that was close to idolatry. So—*death!*

There was no time to snatch the gun from Ram Singh's hand, no time even to knock the muzzle aside. There was one chance only and Wentworth's rapier-keen mind leaped to the solution. His fist snaked out with the speed and velocity of a striking cobra. The blow caught Ram Singh upon the jaw and wrenched him into instant unconsciousness. The gun dropped from his hand, blasted its bullet harmlessly into the floor.

Wentworth stooped and recovered the weapon, stood gazing on Ram Singh. He did not for a moment question the man's loyalty to himself. And other than that, there could be no blot upon the Sikh's honor. When he had revived Ram Singh, he told him that gravely, almost as a man might speak to a child.

"There shall be a vengeance," Wentworth promised. "Only cowards seek a coward's way out. And thou art a lion among warriors, Singh!"

Wentworth swung from Ram Singh's room, confident he had averted any possibility of suicide, and found Jackson waiting almost on the threshold, too discreet to appear to have overheard.

"Mr. Kirkpatrick on the telephone, sir," Jackson reported stolidly. "He says it's urgent!"

Wentworth strode swiftly to the phone. Stanley Kirkpatrick was his oldest friend, was sometimes his fiercest enemy. For Kirkpatrick was the commissioner of the city police, and there had been times in his Underworld battles when Wentworth had been forced to step outside the law. But those excursions into crime were never proved, and until they were, Kirkpatrick and Wentworth fought side by side.

Kirkpatrick's voice rushed at him and Wentworth understood that he was not to interrupt, that there was much to say in too short a time.

Kirkpatrick said harshly, "Dick, guard yourself. I have been framed for murder! And it looks like they'll be sure to convict me!"

CHAPTER 2
THE THIRD BLOW

WENTWORTH DID not waste words in protest as most men might have done. He accepted Kirkpatrick's estimate of the situation at face value, and his brain flew beyond the swift details that were poured into his ear. This first blow, the attack upon Ram Singh which had deprived him of all ready cash, except a small amount in a secret safe at his home, might be merely the work of clever thieves. Wentworth doubted that, but it was possible. This attack upon Kirkpatrick could mean only one thing. His apprehensions of the morning, which Nita had so strangely shared, were fully realized! Some new and great mind was marshaling the Underworld for future warfare upon mankind!

Wentworth knew an abrupt certainty that this swift succession of blows had not yet reached their climax. Wentworth, as a fighter of crime, had no peer unless it be Kirkpatrick. Wentworth had been stripped of wealth; Kirkpatrick, who was the greatest commissioner of police the city had ever known, was put out of the fight on a trumped-up murder charge; the next step....

"Make them wait there for you, Kirk," Wentworth broke in swiftly. "I'll be there inside of ten minutes and somehow we'll smash this frame-up!"

"I'll delay action as long as possible," Kirkpatrick said more slowly, "if you think it wise to come. Personally, it looks like a skirmish in a long campaign. You would do better to stand clear, to try to fathom the strategy...."

"Their strategy is to remove you and me!" Wentworth cut in strongly. "We'll prevent part of that right now. *Wait!*"

Kirkpatrick rushed a few more details at him. He was accused of killing a policeman named Blair who had served as his official secretary. He had, in fact, had the man at his apartment working late when he was shot down. Kirkpatrick had heard the shot, rushed into his office. The police who always guarded his outer door had followed and found Kirkpatrick over the body, the murder gun in his hand, and, somewhere close at hand, Kirkpatrick's own voice had seemed to say with calm and cold satisfaction, "Do you think you can rat to officials now, Blair?"

Oscar Dodgington, the prosecuting attorney, had the full case already and was crowing in anticipation of victory. "He's got his office full of newspaper men," Kirkpatrick said wearily. "He's shouting about corruption in public office. It seems that Blair called him up just before he was killed and hinted that he wanted to reveal that I was dealing with criminals, taking money from them, so Dodgington says. It's a hell of a mess, Dick."

Wentworth said firmly, "We'll smash it, Kirk."

The receiver dashed with a sound like a shot as Wentworth wheeled away from the phone.

"Jackson!" he called dearly. "Have the Daimler brought to the door at once!"

He paced grimly to his personal quarters. The Daimler was completely armored, with bullet-proof glass, heavy plate, protected tires. There was armament for a siege in its hidden compartments. Within its locked doors he would be safe enough on his trip to police headquarters. Once there... Methodically, he was checking over two automatics, heavy forty-five caliber weapons which he could use with deadly accuracy. There was an urgency upon him which made his cheeks rigid, which sped the movements of his fingers.

He thrust the weapons into twin holsters beneath his arms, pivoted to leave. The Daimler still had not arrived and, hat and cane tucked under one arm, he delayed by the telephone.

The loss of half a million dollars was serious enough, God knew, but it had additional sinister implications. It might be awkward to raise fresh funds at this time because of the weakness of many others of his holdings. His sharpened faculties seemed to perceive a concerted attack upon all facets of his fortune. His business affairs were largely in the hands of a keen young attorney named Himman. It was up to him to convert some of Wentworth's holdings into ready cash... Himman could not be reached, but Wentworth left the order and hurried from his penthouse.

OUTSIDE THE door of his apartment, two armed guards saluted, holding guns in their left hands. "No trace, sir, of any stranger in the building," they reported. These advices followed Wentworth all the way to the street. Reluctantly, he lifted the state of siege into which he had thrown the building.

At the outer doorway, Jackson stepped forward, his shoulders seeming broader with the alertness that gripped him. An Army automatic hung low in a holster against his side.

"Fall in the guard," he ordered curtly, and the uniformed men Wentworth had placed about the building formed a square about him in which he moved to the Daimler at the curb. Jackson was before him, snapping open the door.

"Suggest an escort, sir," he said bluntly.

Wentworth shook his head. It would cause delay and he must reach police headquarters quickly if he were to see Kirkpatrick before they took him away. He must learn more intimately the details of his friend's dilemma… A heavy frown settled between his brows as the armored doors, swinging shut, were automatically locked. Jackson sprang to the wheel and the Daimler spurted from the curb.

Despite his abstraction, the deep puzzle of the situation, Wentworth kept a keen lookout. It seemed unlikely that any attack would be made on his rolling fortress, yet… It was Wentworth who first saw the convergence of trucks ahead of them.

"Trap, Jackson!" he snapped.

Jackson stood on the brakes, swerved left around the rear

THE COMING OF THE TERROR

of the outer truck with horn blasting. There was a skid, a lurch and the Daimler was clear. Its speed accelerated. The Daimler bore special police symbols and traffic split for the car. The second attempt came without any warning at all. A taxicab cruising on their left cut in abruptly and tangled with the left front wheel. At the same moment a second car spurted front a parking place beside the curb. The converging cars wedged the Daimler. Jackson slammed into second, rammed the gas pedal to the floor. The taxi recoiled from the crash, spun crazily about and locked with a street car moving in the opposite direction. A wrench of the wheel took the Daimler almost clear of the second machine—and a truck ahead of them deliberately backed into the Daimler's nose!

Wentworth's scowl had left his face. In its place was a cool smile. He palmed his two automatics and peered about for the beginning of the attack. A crowd had gathered instantly; auto horns behind made a raucous clamor. Ahead of them, the exhaust pipe of the truck gusted blue clouds of smoke over the scene, but not thickly enough to form a screen. Then Wentworth whipped forward in his seat. That hot, metallic odor! Good God, was the Daimler on fire?

Jackson caught up a fire extinguisher from beside the front seat, bent and ripped at the floor-boards of the car. Deliberately, Wentworth cranked open a narrow gun port in the window beside him. Then he waited for the attack. He heard the hissing operation of the fire extinguisher, was aware that the hot odor had turned sickish and sweet. For a split-second it puzzled him, then his voice cracked sharply.

17

RICHARD WENTWORTH

"Out of the car, Jackson!" he cried. "Shoot on suspicion. That sweet smell… *gas!*"

AS HE shouted, he was unlocking the door on his left.

Together, he and Jackson hit the pavement. Outside, the odor was thicker, more nauseous. In a car just behind them, a man and woman bad slumped down unconscious in their seats. A newsboy, running to see the excitement, was staggering. He leaned against a stationary car and retched, sank slowly to the ground. And as yet there was no enemy in sight! The men who had driven the cars which wrecked the Daimler had fled into the gathering crowd. A whirling dizziness was in Wentworth's brain. Beside him, Jackson staggered and almost fell. Wentworth threw an arm about him, reeled on in retreat.

Half the width of the street lay between them and the wrecked car, but the odor of the gas clung persistently. Wentworth thought dimly, "This is the third blow." He felt his legs go robbery beneath him, but still he clung to his guns, still their muzzles quested about hungrily. He shouted abruptly, challengingly. Toward him, through the dimness of his senses, a man was running.

Wentworth's right hand gun steadied, he almost squeezed the trigger, but he hesitated. He had no way of knowing whether this was one of his assailants, or... It was a man in police blue! Crazy

laughter bubbled from Wentworth's lips. His mind seemed abruptly cold and deliberate, but his body would not obey. He ordered his gun to remain warily on guard and it slipped from his fingers to the street. He ordered his body to arise to its feet and became aware that his cheek was pressing into the hot asphalt of the sun-drenched pavement! He knew that, felt hands lifting him, and knew no more.

From somewhere near, a clock began to chime. It was a quarter of three o'clock.

In a car three blocks away, a hawk-faced man listened to a softly tuned short wave radio. He nodded and a slight smile touched the thinness of his long, mobile lips.

"It is well!" murmured Tang-akhmut, the Man from the East "Proceed with the Plan."

WITH THE stir of returning consciousness, Wentworth knew an immense lassitude, but that was purely physical. His mind flew about swiftly, urgent with the necessity of reaching Kirkpatrick, of determining who among the crowd were his assailants. And then he realized that there was no crowd, that about him was a vast quiet. His eyes flicked open and he stared at a ceiling tinted delicately pink. He roiled, pushed heavily up from the floor. It was white; a deep-pile carpet, and the automatic in his fist made a flat black impression. He surged to his feet and somewhere a voice that he recognized dimly as his own spoke savagely:

"That will teach you to threaten me," it said strangely. "That will teach you to try to rat on me!"

From near by, a woman screamed and Wentworth looked up

slowly toward the sound. A maid in a neat black uniform stood in the doorway. With one stiff arm, she was pointing at him. Her other fist was pressed into her mouth. A  cord that had been binding about Wentworth's temples snapped and he could hear and see clearly. He saw the maid turn and run, heard a pounding at a not-distant door. And then he looked down at the white carpet again. What he saw froze him in his tracks. The carpet was stained with a fresh crimson that could be only blood—and crumpled there was the twisted body of a girl!

Awkwardly, Wentworth dropped on a knee beside her; his hand went to her throat and confirmed his suspicion. The girl was dead! That ripping tear in the tender flesh of her breast had been made by a heavy caliber bullet. But, good God, what was he doing here beside this murdered woman with a gun in his hand? That voice he had heard had seemed to be his own!

With a low cry, Wentworth sprang to his feet. It was all achingly clear to him now. Kirkpatrick had been framed for murder and now Wentworth shared his fate! He and Jackson had been anesthetized in a gas attack—good God, where was Jackson now?—and he had been planted here beside this dead woman whom he did not know, though her fresh young beauty was dimly familiar to him. That voice he had heard had not been his own, but a clever imitation. But the maid had heard it, would tell police....

The police! He heard the sharp, rapid beat of footsteps along the hallway, the maid's excited voice.

"He's still in there, officer!" she cried. "He murdered her. Oh, I know she's dead!"

Wentworth threw a frantic look about him, glimpsed the open door of the bathroom, a closet. The windows were open and the rising pressure of a breeze kited the curtains slightly. The only other exit to the room was the one in which the maid had stood, toward which she ushered a policeman at this moment! Wentworth's brain was working keenly enough now for all the dullness caused by the after-effects of the gas. As the policeman neared the door, he lifted his automatic and fired a shot past the lintel, too high to have injured anyone even had they thrust into the opening at that exact instant.

"You'll never take me alive!" Wentworth shouted, making his voice thin and excited. He fired again, then lifted the automatic toward his own head. He aimed carefully above it, still shouting. "You'll never take me alive! *I'll kill myself!*"

On the heels of the last word, he squeezed the trigger again, collapsed carefully to the white rug so that his head lay in the spreading red stain. As he struck the floor, the policeman charged through the door, revolver in hand. The man lifted up on his toes with the suddenness of his halt. His revolver sagged in his hand and Wentworth realized with a start he scarcely suppressed that this was one of the policemen who had a beat past his own apartment house—Tom Callahan.

"Glory be to God!" gasped Callahan. "It's Mr. Wentworth!"

At his elbow, the maid said, "Yes, yes. Of course it is. Hasn't he been coming to see the mistress these three months…?"

The frame-up was painfully clear to Wentworth, and this poor dead girl on the floor beside him was a sacrifice to the plans of this strange new enemy who struck so terribly.

"Get an ambulance!" Callahan cried, his voice hoarse. The maid turned and ran, and Callahan hurried toward Wentworth. "Glory be to God!" he whispered again. He went down on his knees and Wentworth, his face twisted painfully at the thing he must do, surged up and struck in the same moment. The blow with the automatic was cautious, calculated. It caught Callahan behind the ear, slumped him unconscious to the floor. But he would not be out for long. Swiftly Wentworth snatched drapes from the windows and bound the policeman, thrust a gag between his teeth.

Through the doorway, along a hall, he could hear the maid's excited voice. "Yes, please hurry! An ambulance! Two people shot…."

She hung up, whirled, and saw Wentworth just behind her. The scream that rose in her throat died there.

"Come," Wentworth said quietly. "You're going with me!"

THE MAID shrank back in terror, but Wentworth seized her firmly by the arm, found a cloak in the hall closet which he threw about her shoulders.

"If you make a sound," Wentworth warned her coldly, "I'll shoot you down, you cold-blooded little murderess!"

In a daze of terror, the maid stumbled along beside Wentworth through the hall crowded with curious people, to the elevator.

"One side," Wentworth ordered roughly. "Come on, break it up and get back to your rooms!"

A jittery man in morning clothes stepped in his path. "What is it, officer?" he cried. "This will ruin me, ruin me!"

"You ought to think of that before you let thugs and their molls get into your apartments!" Wentworth said harshly. "Come along now!" He thrust the maid into the elevator. Silently, he cursed the slowness with which he descended. He had the maid momentarily cowed, but there was no telling how long it would last. She might burst into hysteria, and he had to get her away from here, had to question her. Whether or not she had a hand in the murder of that girl, she had deliberately lied about him. She might know Jackson's fate.

They made the doorway, found a taxi-cab, and Wentworth thrust the girl into it. They got away a bare half-minute ahead of the first rocketing police radio roadsters. In a few minutes more, when Tom Callahan had been revived, there would be a general alarm out for Richard Wentworth: "Wanted for murder. Take no chances with this man. He is armed and dangerous!" Wentworth had heard it too many times before to have any doubts of the message! And Kirkpatrick would not be at headquarters to tell his officers how mad the thing they charged could be. Kirkpatrick… Wentworth had failed his friend in his hour of greatest need. Kirkpatrick's words came racingly back to him. "I have been framed for murder. And it looks like they'll be able to convict me!"

The echo of those words went with Wentworth as the taxi tooled an aggressive path through traffic. With it died all thought of remaining to fight the charge against himself. Callahan had identified him beside the body of the dead girl. He turned fiercely to the maid beside him.

"You lied to the police officer," he said coldly. "Why?"

The maid stared at him with her eyes strained wide, a frightened whiteness in her cheeks. Wentworth shook her a little.

"You said I had been coming to see that girl for the last three months," he went on. "You knew that was a lie! Who paid you...?"

The girl broke into stammering speech. "Oh, no sir! I wouldn't lie about a thing like that! Why, sir, I've taken your hat and stick three and four times a week all through those three months. I couldn't be mistaken, sir! And last night, Miss Duncombe said you had told her the most exciting thing about yourself!" The maid's composure broke to bits. Tears welled down her cheeks and sound swelled out her cheeks and popped out through her lips—screams of grief, crazy laughter. Wentworth shook her, saw the taxi driver peering at him suspiciously.

WHAT BIT into Wentworth's consciousness was that the maid was absolutely sincere in what she said. Damn it, she *believed* that he had been calling on that girl, Duncombe, for the last three months! There was only one answer to that. Someone posing as himself, and doing it with a shrewd ability that completely deceived the maid, probably her mistress also, had deliberately built up to this murder and the resultant frame-up! It was damnably well planned, even to the "exciting revelation"

25

of the night before, followed by this murder, to the cry that the Duncombe girl had threatened to "rat" on him. There was build-up, motive, opportunity, even the weapon in his hand. To make matters worse, he had been forced to strike down the arresting officer in order to escape long enough to learn his position in the frame-up. He had hoped the maid was a party to the frame-up, that he could force her secrets from her.

A harsh curse escaped his lips. The plot was sound, and for the present inescapable. He had no choice except to flee into hiding until such time as he could smash the frame-up. Luckily, he had arranged with his business manager, Himman, to get together some ready cash. He leaned forward.

"Stop at the next corner, driver," he said curtly.

The driver passed the next corner with mounting speed. "Like hell, mister!" he called back over his shoulder. "We're going to a cop! That girl...."

Wentworth laid the barrel of his automatic on the back of the front seat. "Pull to the curb!" he instructed quietly.

With a yelp of fright, the driver stopped. He was instantly out of the cab, yelling, shouting for the police.

His excitement set off the maid's hysteria again. Cursing, Wentworth sprang to the pavement, ducked into a corner cigar store. If he was lucky, it would have two exits, and for the moment he could escape the pursuit. For the moment, yes, but within an hour at the most, the police would be hard on his heels again with the entire force of the press and public opinion hounding them to his capture and conviction! Slipping out of the side door and joining in the rushing crowd which thronged toward the shrill screams around the corner, Wentworth had a moment of bitter hatred for the man who was behind this shrewd series of attacks. Months of planning must have gone into the work, and then—

Almost subconsciously, Wentworth glanced at his watch, and he started. It had been two o'clock when Ram Singh had fallen. Since that time, a murder frame-up had been hung on Kirkpatrick, and he himself had been overpowered on the streets and made a fugitive from justice in another murder frame-up which he could not conceivably fight now. He was bereft of funds, unless Himman could produce at once. A slow and grudging respect forced its way through Wentworth's anger, a keen, fierce desire to come to grips with the power behind this shrewd planning. But it was more than that. Surely, no criminal power would dare to strike down those two fierce soldiers of justice, Kirkpatrick and Wentworth, unless there was more, much more and worse, to come! Undoubtedly, this power was clearing the path for crimes beside which the robbery this morning, the frame-ups, would be trivial! Wentworth's fists clenched. He must strike back—and quickly! But where, and at whom was he to direct his attack?

The screaming of the maid had stopped. Wentworth turned away with the crowd and made for the nearest subway entrance.

It was two minutes after five o'clock.

CHAPTER 3
SOLD OUT!

A S A precaution, when he reached his apartment house, Wentworth avoided the main entrance and went to a small, securely locked rear door to which he alone had the key. This door gave into the service entrance of the building, and to the slow and heavy service elevator. A few moments later he let himself into the tradesman's door of his penthouse. Inside, he stood listening acutely. He doubted that the police would have sent searchers here for him as yet.

Ram Singh, his hurts bandaged, domed in the fresh white that was his habit, met him in the hallway with a low salaam. "Pardon thy servant's madness, *sahib*," he murmured, his strong voice harshly self-accusatory.

Wentworth nodded a quick acceptance. "Has Himman called here yet?" he demanded quickly, "or sent any message?"

"*Han, sahib,*" Ram Singh said humbly, "the Himman *sahib* is here now. In the *sahib's* study. The Hospital of Mercy phoned, *sahib*. Jackson is there, not seriously hurt, they said."

With a sharp exclamation of pleasure, Wentworth hastened along the hallway, bounded up the stairs to the second floor of his duplex, where he maintained a small study whose walls were lined with the books he loved, yet so rarely had time to study. He whipped into the room.

"How much could you raise, Himman?" he asked quickly. There was an urgency in him, a need for swift action. He must flee these quarters, set up others, strike the trail of his enemy.

Himman jumped up—a young, worried man with scowling brows. "Mr. Wentworth, I—" He hesitated. "I don't know how to tell you, sir."

Wentworth felt again the swift presentiment of disaster. Good God, was he so helpless that the enemy hammered at him at will, a man with his guard down, at the mercy of his opponent? What was this new blow? He forced himself to calmness.

"Out with it, Himman," he said curtly. "What are you talking about?"

Himman shrugged, spread out his palms. "Your bank, sir," he said in agitation. "The examiners are there. It won't open its doors in the morning!"

Wentworth cursed slowly, quietly. This was more damnable than the other blows. An innocent girl had been killed in order to snare him, but through the closing of that bank hundreds of depositors would suffer!

"This is deadly serious, Himman," he said. "I will throw what resources I can into the bank, try to save it. But surely the failure of that one bank...."

Himman's eyes were still on his face. There was trepidation in his manner. "No, Mr. Wentworth," he said slowly, "that one bank would not ruin you, even though you are its major stockholder. But you know that almost every stock you hold has been under a merciless pounding recently. It is almost as if there was somebody out to get you in the market. Your account is largely discretional, and many of the better stocks were posted as collateral to hold the others."

A COLD and angry calm was settling upon Wentworth. His

29

gray-blue eyes bored into those of his manager. "Don't be so circuitous," he said shortly. "Come to the point. My stocks, I gather, are sold out! The bank in which I keep most of my cash, for whose stock I am liable to assessment, has failed! What else? I seem to remember something like two million dollars in government bonds which you have placed in deposit somewhere for me. I don't suppose the government has failed, too?"

Himman wet his lips with facile tongue. He spread his hands. "You won't believe what I have to tell you, Mr. Wentworth. I thought of those government bonds first thing when the bank closed. I went to the deposit vault where they are kept, and… Mr. Wentworth, God help me, it isn't my fault! *Every one of those bonds has been stolen!*"

Wentworth felt a slow and hard rigidity creep down his arms. His fists knotted, but his voice was very quiet. "What else?" he asked softly. "I own a majority of the stock in the Besselmark Steel Company. That would not have… Good God, Himman, talk! Can't you understand…."

Himman swallowed hard. "Mr. Wentworth, the company is being forced into receivership! I was just notified of the action before I came here this afternoon. Mr. Wentworth, sir… God help us both… you are ruined!"

Wentworth took a slow step forward and Himman shrank back. He got his shoulders against the wall and thrust out his hands defensively. He began to chatter, so frightened that his words were unintelligible. Wentworth controlled himself with an effort, his eyes piercing in his anger. There was something incredibly wrong here—not alone his financial ruin. It was the perfect timing of the whole action. Stripped of his wealth, a fugitive… There were still valuables on which he could realize, but it would take time, and a fugitive from the law could not wait on such matters. But how had these things been so subtly arranged that he'd had no hint beforehand of what impended? A slow and burning suspicion crawled through his mind.

"Would you tell me, please," he said with enforced calm, "why I was kept in ignorance of this crisis? Will you tell me also what you were doing while these things were developing? It seems to me that I pay you a salary of twenty-five thousand dollars a year to manage my affairs." A sudden thought stopped him. His voice became terribly still. "Is it possible, Himman, that you *sold me out!*"

Himman's lips trembled. He moistened them again. "I resent that," he blustered. "I resent that, Mr. Wentworth. You know I wouldn't sell you out. You are making an imputation against my integrity!"

Wentworth laughed with a sharp, rasping intensity. "I am ruined, is that it, Himman? All the possessions I have are value-less or else entailed for debts. I suppose, also—"

With fingers that trembled slightly, Himman drew a blue-backed legal paper from an inner pocket "I was compelled to accept service, sir," he said weakly. "The bank examiners wanted to be sure of protection on your assessment for stock!"

Wentworth stared at Himman through a long minute, then he moved toward him, slowly, quietly. "This is not vengeance, Himman," he said. "I could not blame you for honest mistakes.

31

I never have. But these mistakes were not honest! Himman, you sold me out!"

He seized the cowering Himman by the threat and closed his thumbs inexorably on the man's windpipe. "Not vengeance, Himman," he whispered again, "but by God you'll tell me who paid you to ruin me, or…" His thumbs increased their pressure. IT TOOK minutes to force Himman to talk, but finally he gasped out hoarse words that were scarcely intelligible… and Wentworth stepped back from him, amazed, stunned by the force of this discovery. Incredulously, he heard the name of the man who had ruined him through this miserable tool.

"But that's impossible," he whispered.

Himman pushed up on an elbow on the floor where he had been flung. "He ruined you!" Himman gasped, "and he'll run you to earth! You cannot escape from *Oscar Dodgington!*"

Dodgington conspire to ruin him? Wentworth shook his head. "You're lying," he said coldly. "Dodgington doesn't hate me. The prosecuting attorney has no reason to strike at me. You're lying…" He stopped then, remembering that Dodgington was the chief mover against Kirkpatrick.

Himman cowered to his feet. "No, no, as God is my witness, Dodgington did it! He said he knew you were a criminal, but you could hire good attorneys and get off. He had to ruin you first, strip you of wealth before he could convict you! He appealed to my civic pride, my… my sense of justice, and—"

"And your pocketbook!"

Wentworth slapped Himman heavily in the mouth. Himman fell and caught his head a glancing blow on a chair arm. He lay motionless where he had fallen and Wentworth stared blankly down at him. Dodgington, long before today's murder frame-up, had maneuvered against him, which meant that Dodgington, so inexorable against Kirkpatrick in the present crisis, was the ally of Wentworth's enemy, the new and overpowering criminal… Savagely, Wentworth forced himself to the realization of what Himman's revelation meant. His eyes took on a chill glow.

Outside the closed door of the study, Wentworth heard the whisper of racing feet. He heard Ram Singh's shout and a woman's swift, anxious reply. He knew that voice and he turned blindly, gropingly, toward the door. In his hour of need, Nita had come to him. The one woman in the world who knew the awful secret of the Spider, who revered and loved him for his thankless service to an ideal. He held out his arms. The door jerked open and Nita van Sloan ran to him. She beat her small white fists on his chest.

"Oh, Dick, hurry, hurry," she cried. "We've got to hurry!"

Wentworth's arms closed about her. He laughed harshly. "Hurry from what?"

"The police are on their way up!" Nita said tensely. "I short-circuited the elevator so they would have to walk. Please, Dick."

"Only the police?" Wentworth asked sharply.

The depths of Nita's violet eyes were troubled. "I saw only police, Dick. Is there something else?"

She leaned back to gaze at him better and became aware of Himman's unconscious form. With a low cry she knelt beside the man and touched a finger to the throat pulse. Her face was relieved as she arose again. "I thought for a moment he was dead! What happened, Dick?"

Coldly, without the least expression in his voice, Wentworth told her. "There is nothing I can do now except run away," he said, his voice choking oddly as he finished.

Nita crept into his arms. "Oh, Dick, Dick lover," she whispered, "what's to become of us now?"

CHAPTER 4
FLIGHT!

GRIMLY, WENTWORTH held Nita close. There was no time to lose, no time even for this final, parting caress. With police and God knew what other enemies on his heels, he had no choice except flight. And it must be alone. Penniless, hunted on every side, he could not involve Nita nor the brave men who had fought beside him in so many battles.

Nita was talking, "... in hiding until you can find out your enemies. My money will be enough to provide for both of us. Only hurry, Dick."

Wentworth's arms tightened about the woman he loved. He dropped his lips to her hair and for a moment drew her closer, then he released her. "That's fine," he told her hurriedly. "As soon as I'm in a safe hiding place, I'll communicate with you." He tried to make his eyes help the deception. She must believe him.

He darted to the door, wrenched it open.

Nita cried after him despairingly. "Dick, Dick, give me your promise!"

Wentworth's lips closed in a tight line as he raced along the hallway toward the service door of the penthouse. She asked a thing he could not do, for the Spider had never broken a promise. And he had no intention of sending for Nita, of forcing her to share the fugitive's life he must lead.

The closing of the service door shut out Nita's voice. Wentworth sprang to the steps that wound downward, rapidly unscrewed a light bulb from a wall bracket and jammed a key into the socket. His arm tingled with the shock, there was a flash of blue light as he accomplished a short circuit and, in the wall, a hidden door whipped open. Calmly, Wentworth screwed the bulb back into place, stepped through the door, closed it again.

This was no haven he had achieved, merely a resting place on his fight to obscurity. He must have weapons and fresh clothing. This hidden room with its two entrances, one into the music room, the other seldom used save in emergency, on the service steps, was small. It held a wall of racked clothing, the implements of the disguises Wentworth sometimes assumed in his battles. The other wall contained a compact chemical laboratory.

Hurriedly, Wentworth washed and put on fresh clothing. He bent for a moment over a dressing table and did swift things to his face: changed the lean tan of his complexion to a ruddy hue; darkened the flesh about his eyes. Putty, skillfully shaped, thickened his nose. That was all that was necessary. When he walked, his carriage would be that of an older man, with the spring gone from his stride. There would be a hopeless cast to his features, a beaten line to his mouth. No man would mistake him for the flashing and brilliant Wentworth. Eyeing himself

35

in the mirror, Wentworth's lips twisted ironically. The identity he was assuming was quite accurate. He had been beaten in a single swift encounter with the enemy! But there would be other encounters—other sharp skirmishes with death. And the Spider had never yet lost a final battle with any foe!

From his discarded clothing, he took out the blue-backed legal paper that Himman had given him. He put it in his pocket, crossed to the door by which he had entered. The service hall was empty, but from below stairs came the shout, the clatter of the police! Wentworth stepped quickly from the secret room, crossed to the main entrance to his penthouse and pressed the

The man dropped his hold on the girl and reached for his gun—but too late.

bell button. Ram Singh wrenched open the door, glared inimically.

"What do you want?" he demanded.

Wentworth assumed an air of insolence. "I have papers to serve on Mr. Wentworth," he said.

Ram Singh stepped reluctantly aside, and Wentworth entered. He was in no danger of challenge by the police. There were a thousand process servers in the city and they were civil actuaries who had no connection with criminal work. Ram Singh's hostility would be his best guarantee against discovery by the police.

Wentworth's disguise proved adequate. The police searched the apartment with a frantic thoroughness, but never thought to examine the process server as their fugitive.

WENTWORTH DARED not look directly at Nita, but he loved the pride in her carriage, the scorn with which she regarded these men who had come for her lover.

The police finally herded him out into the street.

He fled through the city, uncertain whether he would be spotted and followed by the enemies who had struck him down. There was in him a fierce determination to strike and strike quickly at this new and rising criminal power. It was possible Dodgington might afford him a clue. Himman, in spite of his terror, might have lied about the prosecuting attorney's activities. Even now, Wentworth found it hard to believe that the stalwart Dodgington would deliberately conspire to frame him for murder, when that frame-up involved the slaughter of an innocent girl.

Nevertheless, he was determined to investigate—and then the evening newspapers slapped him in the face. With the single exception of a minor paper, operated by a personal friend, they were unanimous in their denunciation of Richard Wentworth. The blatant sheets described the girl, Iris Duncombe, as Wentworth's mistress. She was, it appeared, a night club dancer and she had been seen frequently in his company during the preceding months. The papers hinted cleverly that she had learned something incriminating against Wentworth, "who on several occasions has been accused by the police of being identical with the murderous Spider!" They made no mention of the fact that whenever those charges had been made, they had subsequently been disproved by Wentworth.

Nor was this the end of the screaming scandal in the news sheets. He and Kirkpatrick were branded together by Dodgington as the "murder twins." People in the streets had been asked by reporters: "Do you believe that Richard Wentworth is the Spider?" The answers were practically unanimous. It was torturing stuff to read. The newspapers inferred cleverly that Iris Duncombe had been in touch with the police, had been on the point of making damaging admissions of information she had gained from Wentworth. And they hinted again and again that this information was to the effect that Richard Wentworth was the Spider, that he had murdered the girl to keep that information from reaching the police. It was cleverly done, so shrewdly in fact that for days Wentworth accepted the hatred and opprobrium of the papers as a true reflection of public sentiment.

He learned that Dodgington had left the city for a brief

rest "preparatory to the prosecution of Kirkpatrick for his dastardly crime," and Wentworth realized that with him went his one opportunity of penetrating the enemy defenses.

PHARAOH ‘Y’ EGYPT

Wentworth lived quietly in the days that followed, swept along by the invariable pressure of existence, eating and sleeping. He took a room in a middle class hotel.

The newspapers thundered at him, the letters-from-the-public columns were full of denunciation.

One newspaper had started a public subscription for a reward to go to the captor of Richard Wentworth, "alias the Spider."

Thousands were contributing… They read avidly the news of the hunt for the Spider and ignored the steadily rising tide of crime which Wentworth discerned. Bank robberies were rapidly increasing, thefts of bonds in Wall Street, payroll hold-ups. The papers were full of that, but it was all crowded into the back pages, away from the front page importance which they gave the news of the hunt for Wentworth. He could not repress his bitterness. Almost, it was as if the Underworld, rejoicing in his misfortune, were celebrating with a saturnalia of crime. Or else the new criminal power was organizing the Underworld into an efficient machine for murder and robbery, had cleared the way for it by destroying Wentworth and Kirkpatrick.

HIS RISING anger drove Wentworth from his room, and as if a jeering destiny were resolved to test him to the uttermost, the path of the Underworld intercepted his. Strolling along empty streets, Wentworth's senses perceived certain signs which he could not mistake. There, across the street, an automobile with its engine quietly running, stood at the curb. Nearby was a darkened alley in which Wentworth knew a light should burn. It ran along the back, the vault side, of a wealthy bank. The man in police uniform who stood at the entrance of the alley would deceive most people, but Wentworth, already acquainted with some of the mannerisms of the new criminal power, was dubious. Undoubtedly, the man in uniform was an impostor. Far from being a member of the law's protective forces, he was the lookout for the criminals even now at work robbing that bank.

For a moment, on his quiet way, Wentworth hesitated, hand creeping toward the gun that nestled beneath his arm. It would be so simple for the Spider, working with his smooth and deadly efficiency, to thwart this looting. A shot into the driver's seat of that car, a second at that uniformed fraud at the entrance of the alley, and the get-away would be stalled. A few hot minutes of gunfight, with the stalled car for a barricade for himself... Wentworth's hand closed on the butt of his automatic. But why should he? What would it profit him? Another crime, more "murders" laid to the Spider's account. They would call them murders when his action would be that of any police officer interfering with a bold robbery!

When Wentworth had fled his penthouse, it was with the determination to learn instantly if the attack on himself and Kirkpatrick had been criminally inspired, to fix upon the guilty man behind such machinations. Kirkpatrick was awaiting trial in the Tombs. Jackson and Ram Singh had been forced to flee

41

into exile lest they be dragged down by the all-devouring wrath against Wentworth, whom they served. No, Wentworth could afford no diversions now from his main task, could not chance a slip-up that might put him out of the game. Deliberately, he strode away from the scene of robbery, returned stolidly to his room. And the next day, the newspapers blamed the Spider for the robbery!

Its cleverness was typical of his work, they said, and a caped and twisted figure that everyone knew was the Spider had been seen near the scene of the crime. He had had accomplices, the account ran on, and then Wentworth's name was brought into the story, and the fact that Jackson and Ram Singh could not be found. They hinted that he would soon need funds to keep in hiding. A bitter curse dragged Wentworth to his feet. A grimness touched the line of his mouth. They said one thing truly. The Spider would soon need funds if he were to remain in hiding. Well, he was already being blamed for crimes of money. And it was truth that the Spider's skill, used so often for others, could help him now. It was not for nothing that he had perfected his ability to open safes!

Wentworth knew of a dozen men who had come by their riches by crooked means. Bitterly, he determined to strike this very night! There was a certain grafting contractor who made his money out of city jobs. He would do as well as any other, for a start. Wentworth knew a certain excitement at the prospect and he smiled sardonically.

But Wentworth's bitterness carried him to an extreme that he would never have considered, had he been less alone, less persecuted. He determined that if the public thought him so vile a criminal they should have at least some justification for that belief. When he robbed tonight, there should be no doubts in the mind of anyone as to who had performed the deed. He would sign and seal it with the crimson emblem of the Spider!

WITHIN AN hour after he had reached the determination to act, Wentworth strolled casually past the contractor's Park Avenue home, one of the few single residences left along its cliff-dweller walls. The survey was almost superfluous. He had once been inside the house and that once was ample to plant all its details in his memory. There was an intricate alarm system, but that only entailed work. Wentworth knew all the makes of alarm systems, knew how they were operated and how to contravent them; just as he knew the mechanics of safes. It had been part of the rigorous training he had set for himself when he had determined on his life as the Spider.

No, none of these things was difficult and finally he stood before the open safe, gazing down at the money he had been able to find in its depths, a scant three thousand dollars. For a man's living, it would be ample. For the Spider, crusading, it would be nothing. Wentworth's mobile lips twisted harshly. Well, there would be no more crusading! The Spider was done with all that, forever. Here, he would plant for the people their justification.

With swift, gloved hands he found a sheet of heavy bond paper and across it, in neat but disguised script, he wrote:

"Received, payment in full for one of your misdeeds to the public—"

He wrote no signature, but drew from his vest pocket a

43

slim platinum cigarette lighter. He thumbed its base open and pressed down firmly upon the receipt. When he had returned the lighter to his pocket, there gleamed from the paper a minia- ture reproduction in scarlet of the avenging creature he had chosen as his namesake, the seal of the Spider! For a while then, Wentworth stood staring down at that symbol of his downfall.

Silent, harsh laughter opened his lips and their line was fierce and mocking. For a moment longer, the Spider stood there, then he heeled about and stole silently away through the dusk.

BACK AT the hotel, Wentworth sped directly to his room. Inside, he paused rigidly, listening. He had not lost his acute senses and they told him that there was a living presence in the dark room!

"Stand as you are!" he ordered harshly.

An automatic flipped into his hand. He switched on the light. Then vision came to his light-blurred eyes and he uttered a choked cry, thrust away his gun. It was Nita! She ran to meet him. Wentworth had a flashing thought that she undoubtedly had been followed by the police, but it was only a thought. Noth- ing mattered at the moment except her warm presence.

"You shouldn't have come, dear," he told her presently when

NITA VAN SLOAN

they sat together on the divan. "Don't you know what it means if you are discovered here?"

Nita shook her head of chestnut curls, smiling faintly. "No police followed me, Dick. I doubled my trail too many times. Finding you wasn't too hard. We had talked over so many times what you would do if this situation ever arose. I knew you'd choose a hotel with at least two exits—and one where the cooking wasn't too terrible. I bribed a detective agency into giving me a card as their agent, and then I looked for your handwriting on the registers."

"Where the cooking isn't too terrible!" Wentworth murmured. "But, Good Lord, Nita, am I as transparent as that? If you can do that, the police…."

Nita laughed softly. "But I have special knowledge!"

Wentworth sprang to his feet and took a quick turn across the room. "You must leave, Nita!" he said grimly. "We both must leave. The danger is too great!"

Nita came after him. "Does danger matter, Dick?" she said quietly. "Do you know what is happening in the city?"

Wentworth stopped his pacing, laughed bitterly. "Yes, I know. Every man, woman and child in it is trying to destroy me!"

"Is that all you know?"

Wentworth whirled to face her. "Isn't it enough? Knowing that, can anything else possibly affect me?"

Nita looked at him curiously. She came close and put her narrow white hands on his chest and gazed deeply into his eyes. "I know it hurts, Dick, but they don't know what they are doing! Surely, you don't expect sanity from a mob?"

The set of Wentworth's jaw grew stubborn. "I don't expect anything, but I know I'm through. They have killed the Spider! Let him stay dead!"

Wentworth's vehemence drove Nita from him. She stood staring at him, her full lower lip caught between her teeth. She shook her head. "You won't say that long, Dick. Listen, I hunted you in the Underworld before I came here. They're talking there. Not much, but what you can hear is enough. There's a new boss criminal at work. They're giving him credit for putting the Spider on the run! They pay tribute to him for every job they pull! And there's another thing that doesn't look just right. A new cult has been started. It's headed by an Oriental of some sort. He might be Chinese except that his eyes are Occidental. He uses a lot of luxurious trappings and I think it's a blind for criminal operations of some sort. The police don't seem to be able to do anything about either of these things."

Wentworth gestured angrily. "You are talking of something that might have interested the Spider. The Spider is dead!"

There was bewilderment in Nita's violet eyes, but there was a curious light there, too. Strangely, it seemed to hint at happiness!

"Oh, Dick, do you mean it?" she whispered. "Do you mean that… you are through with these endless battles? If you do…."

Wentworth gazed tenderly down into her eyes. Nita had fought valiantly beside him through years of struggle with the Underworld, rarely voicing the hope that was ever present in both their hearts: the hope that someday the battle would be finished, that then they might marry and have a home of their

47

own, all the things that were denied them now. That hope had grown very faint in recent months, but now....

Wentworth took Nita's shoulders and shook her slightly. "Darling, I am a fugitive from the police! There are many rewards out for me, including the one my dear public has subscribed!"

"I don't care!" Nita cried. "They'll never find you!" She laid her head against his breast. "They won't find you, Dick. Haven't we this right to happiness? Oh, haven't we earned it... The police are stupid. They'll never...."

Nita's voice froze in her throat. She stiffened, staring at the door, and the knock came again, hard, peremptory, challenging. Slowly, Wentworth put Nita away from him, slipped an automatic from an under-arm holster and put it into his coat pocket. He kept his hand on it.

"Who is it?" he asked shortly.

The voice that answered was suave, mocking. "Scarcely a polite greeting, my friend," the man said. "I know who you are—and I bring you a message from the Boss!"

CHAPTER 5
SPIDER BAIT

WENTWORTH'S EYES flew questioningly to Nita, then returned to the door. Nita had said that this new criminal leader demanded tribute on every job. Tonight, Wentworth had robbed a safe and already the collector of the Boss, as the Underworld called him, was at his door! But he was conjecturing... Deliberately, head pulled down so that he stared forward under his brows, Wentworth opened the door. He stood in the opening, hand on pocket gun.

"I don't know your boss," he said quietly, "and I'm not interested in your message…."

He broke off. His fist closed on the man's lapels, jerked him inside the room and hurled him to his knees. Wentworth's movements as he drew his automatic seemed deliberate, but the gun was presented in an incredibly brief second. Its muzzle yawned in the face of the messenger of the Boss.

"Well," Wentworth prompted softly, "I'm waiting."

The man was not disconcerted. His was a smooth, moon-like face on which no trace of beard was discernible. His hat had jarred from his head and showed him completely bald, the scalp gleaming and polished. Wentworth thought he detected a lurking smile in the man's impassive green eyes. Abruptly, Nita was at his side, her fingers gouging into his arm.

"This is the head of that cult!" she whispered fiercely. Her voice grew scornful. "He calls himself the Lama of Love."

Wentworth studied the man as he rose deliberately from his knees and stooped for his hat. When it was on his head, it perched ridiculously, an incongruous thing. Orientals rarely could wear western headgear properly. Wentworth's eyes narrowed and he spat out a string of guttural, rasping sounds. For a moment, the green eyes of his prisoner widened, then the suave smile returned to his lips.

Wentworth nodded. "As I thought, a Tibetan. You have strayed far from your native hills, O Lama of Love!"

The man bowed imperturbably. "My master is served by men

from the four corners of the earth. I bring a double message from him. He commands his tribute, fifty percent of the three thousand you stole tonight. In return, he promises immunity from prosecution. The second message"—the

smooth-faced one bowed—"bids you to the Presence!"

Wentworth laughed harshly. "I need no promises, thou turtle! I pay no tribute—" he stepped nearer, his mien menacing—"and I obey no orders! Do I make myself clear?"

The Tibetan bowed, walked stolidly toward the door. His silence, his equable acceptance of the defiance, were more menacing than any verbal threat. When he was gone, Wentworth and Nita stared at each other.

"You're apparently right about the combination of the cult and this Boss," Wentworth said and laughed scornfully. "Lama of Love!"

Nita whispered, "I'm afraid! He found you so easily! He knew what you had done, even the amount you stole!"

"Coincidence," Wentworth said impatiently. "I left a receipt in the safe and evidently the Boss' men made a later foray."

Nita shuddered. "That man is so evil! Oh, Dick, let us leave the country!"

Wentworth did not answer, but silently paced the room, eyes intent on the floor. Unbidden, the urge to battle was rising within him, but he would not listen to it. Why should he risk Nita's and his own life in warfare against this new criminal menace? His only reward would be new indictment, new hatred from the public. He stopped, staring rigidly with unseeing eyes. For the first time, it seemed, he realized fully that there could be no return to the old life. His penthouse, his valiant aides were gone forever. The eye of suspicion was turned upon Jackson and Ram Singh and, at their first move to help him, they would be seized. He was doomed, by the people he had served, to live out his life an outlaw, a wanted man with a heavy price on his head! And Nita....

She crept into his arms. "Oh, Dick, I am so afraid!"

WENTWORTH SHOOK off his inactivity. The only remedy was flight. Long ago, he had planted funds in Europe for just such use as this. He and Nita could run away....

In the hallway, he heard a girl cry out sharply. The rising scream was instantly strangled. Feet thudded on the carpeted floors.

Wentworth's lips set stubbornly, everything in him urged that he go to that girl's assistance. A sob reached his ears. With a curse, Wentworth darted to the door. To refrain from battling the Boss was one thing; to permit a crime to be committed almost before his eyes was another. That girl's cry had been frightened, piteous... He whipped open the door. Two men in the garb of laundry truck workers had lifted the helpless girl and were placing her in one of the small hand trucks used to collect soiled linen. She was not gagged, but unconscious. The two men whipped about at sight of Wentworth. One of them drew a gun in a swiftly fluid movement.

"Keep out of this, buddy!" he warned.

Wentworth looked again at the girl. She was the hotel attendant who worked at the cigar counter in the lobby. She had often decried down the Spider in his hearing. Bitterness touched Wentworth. This girl had called the Spider crook and murderer. Now only the Spider stood between her and the will of these men. He shrugged his shoulders. That did not matter now. He could not permit this open abduction....

"Okay, okay," he said swiftly to the gunman. "No hard feelings, see. I just heard the dame squeal and I...."

As he had hoped, Nita entered the battle. Through the half-open door, she hurled a cigarette tray. Her aim was true and the heavy glass caught the forehead of the man who had drawn his gun. He staggered, his gun jerking up wildly. In that breath of time, Wentworth acted. A single long bound brought him within reach of the two. He struck first at the man who still held the girl's shoulders. The man dropped his hold, tried for his gun, and was too late. Wentworth's automatic thudded against his temple. A whirl, a second lashing blow and the dazed gunman Nita had struck also fell unconscious to the floor.

Without hesitation, Wentworth dumped the two men into the linen truck, threw a soiled sheet over them, then snatched up the girl. Nita threw wide the door of his room and he bolted through.

"Revive her!" Wentworth snapped as he laid the girl on the bed. He raced back to the hall, seized the linen truck and rolled

The silenced rifle spat and the bullet thudded into the Negro's body.

it also into his room. His heart was beating strongly; a fierce pleasure in the action pulsed through him. But what a fool he was, throwing himself into a battle with crooks at a time like this! And now he had the unconscious girl on his hands….

Even while the thought raced through his brain, his competent hands were at work. He bound and gagged the two men, set to work to revive the girl. It was soon apparent that she had been drugged and Wentworth located the needle prick on her arm. He straightened, his lips set. He had planned to set the girl free, leave the men prisoner and flee from the hotel with Nita. That wasn't possible now. He couldn't leave the helpless girl. He stood looking down at her unconscious form. Her face, relaxed by the drugs, was almost child-like. Her lips had a soft, trusting curve. A curse exploded from Wentworth.

"All right," he said shortly, "we'll have to—wear the men's uniforms, Nita. Just pull them on over your clothes. The hallways won't be brightly lighted at this time of night and we can pass."
THEN THEY had donned the striped denim uniforms. Wentworth thrust the still unconscious men into the closet, laid the girl in the linen basket. Then he and Nita wheeled the truck into a hallway, rang the bell of the service elevator…. The operator of the cage glanced at them incuriously and they reached the laundry truck in the hotel inner court without trouble. It was the work of moments to stow the girl in the back, to start the motor and jolt out into the street. Once under way, Wentworth turned wearily to Nita.

"A new crime of the Spider," he said bitterly. "The Boss will notify the police that I was in that room. The two men will tell how they tried to prevent me from kidnapping the girl and were knocked out by the Spider and his woman accomplice. Only they'll call you a moll, won't they, Nita? The Spider's gun moll. Luckily they won't know I'm Richard Wentworth. I still wear disguise." He laughed in self-mockery.

Nita touched his arm. "Bitterness isn't becoming in you, Dick," she said quietly. "What do you care what they say so long as you know that you have saved the girl? Pretty little thing, isn't she? What do you suppose they wanted with her?"

Wentworth drove grimly on. He sought the open country, a side-lane where they could park unobserved. There, once more he set about reviving the girl. Apparently she had had only a light dose of narcotic, for she soon became conscious. As the dazing effects of the drug diminished, she stared at Wentworth and Nita. There was pride and anger in her dark gaze.

"You can do what you please with me," she said defiantly. "I won't tell where he is!"

Nita removed the uniform cap that hid her dark curls, smiled gently down at the girl. "We don't want you to tell anything, dear," she said. "Two men were trying to kidnap you and we stopped them."

The girl peered more closely into their faces, then relaxed with a sigh. She smiled at Wentworth. "Yes, I remember now. You are a guest at the hotel. We had a little... argument one time about... the Spider!"

Wentworth laughed. "Yes," he said quietly. "What do you think of the Spider now?"

The girl stared at him wonderingly. "I don't understand," she said. She lay back with her eyes closed, her face very pale. Sleep was her greatest need now to allow the final effects of the drug to wear off. In a few moments her deep breathing made a gentle rhythm. Wentworth turned, frowning, to Nita.

"They'll be looking for us in this truck," he said, his voice strangely harsh. "I think we can leave the girl safely."

Nita did not look at him. "Yes, Dick."

She left the truck then without question and they walked steadily, side by side, along the lane toward the main road. They stopped once to discard the uniforms, stopped again when Wentworth peered back along the lane.

"She's all right," he muttered. "Just have to sleep off the effects of the drug. She can go into hiding with whoever she is protecting from the crooks."

Nita said, "Yes, Dick." There was a secret smile on her lips. How well she knew this man of hers!

THEY REACHED the main road and stood waiting. But it would be folly to ask for a ride while darkness lasted, and by daylight they must be far away. Wentworth scowled into the fading night. "Why don't you say something?" he demanded harshly. "Why don't you tell me I'm running away from my duty?"

Nita smiled slightly again, and didn't look at him. There was a warmth and a wistfulness, too, about her lips. "Why call it duty?" she said. "She's one of those who hate the Spider. "Let her fight her own battles—or go to the police."

"The police!" Wentworth said savagely. "The Boss controls them! He must. He offered me protection and he would have to make good on that if he offered it to crooks. Otherwise, they would collect with bullets!"

Nita laughed softly. "What are you arguing about, Dick?" She faced him and a reluctant smile began to tug at Wentworth's lip corners, too.

"I'm a fool, Nita," he said finally.

Nita nodded, "You are, Dick."

"But I can't leave that kid alone to fight the crooks. She wouldn't stand a chance, Nita."

"No, Dick."

Wentworth stared off toward the east where there was a single silver bar of light that heralded the dawn. He said slowly, "It doesn't matter what she thinks of me. She needs… the Spider!"

Nita turned without a word and started back along the lane toward the laundry truck and Wentworth's step beside her was suddenly light. He hummed softly under his breath. His bitterness was gone. He realized that he was quite happy.

"No, it doesn't matter what she thinks of me," he said again. "It's what I think of myself that counts!"

Nita stumbled on the overgrown path, clutched at Wentworth's arm. Her eyes were blurred and the laughter in her throat was half tears. It wasn't even what he thought of himself that mattered, she knew. It was the fact that the girl was alone and helpless. Without his great heart, Richard Wentworth would never have become the Spider, whom men called merciless and a murderer. He had been bitter, sulking for a while, for he was sensitive as all kind men must be. And Nita realized something else; that her Dick would never quit the battle while life was in him. He could not be true to himself and turn his back on the people who needed him, no matter how they repaid his service.

When they came presently to the truck they had abandoned in the woods lane, the girl they had returned to succor ran to meet them, sobbing. Nita folded her in hers arm and, over her head, her eyes met Wentworth's. He smiled and turned away toward the truck. This was recompense enough, his heart cried, the glory in Nita's eyes.

Presently, Nita led the girl to the truck and Wentworth spoke gruffly. "I'm going to help you if you'll let me," he said. "But before either of us says any more, I am the Spider! I thought you ought to know."

The girl stared at him with widening eyes and a rigid gravity spread over Wentworth's face. "I don't care what you think of me," he began harshly, "but if I'm going to help...."

The girl seized his hand eagerly. "Oh, but I think you're wonderful!" she cried. "I've always worshipped you, and..." She stopped at the puzzlement in Wentworth's eyes. "You mean... the things I said at the hotel? I had to say them. I was under orders of..." Her voice died and the light went out of her eyes.

Nita grinned at Wentworth, a gamin grin that mocked him. She was deriding his bitterness against this girl, hinting that perhaps all the outcry against the Spider was similarly inspired, for it was clear she was about to add "the orders of—the Boss!" Nita touched the girl's shoulder then with a gentle hand.

"Don't you understand, dear?" she said. "He wants to help you."

THE GIRL'S apprehension burst from her in a storm of tears.

When it had subsided, she told her story with a pitiful brevity, a hopelessness that moved Wentworth deeply. Her name was Beth Robertson. Her father had been discharged from a life-time position by a new manager of the office where he worked and had, in vengeance and to support her, embezzled money. In some way unknown to her, a man who was called the Boss had penetrated their hiding place.

Since then she had obeyed his orders lest her father be turned over to the authorities. Twice, she and her father had fled and changed their names, but it seemed to make no difference. They were found again. Yesterday, they had agreed that her father would slip away while she was at work. He would wear women's clothes which she had gotten together for him and they would try once more… And the kidnapers had come for her! She turned hopefully to Wentworth.

"It looks as if father got away," she said, "because they came after me. Oh, do you think you can help us to get away, Spider?"

A slight smile touched Wentworth's lips. It would have been so simple a few weeks ago to rid these two of all terror. Ample funds could do so much, and now he had so little—only the three thousand he had stolen. There was no telling when he would be able to find so much again. Still, he must divide with Beth Robertson and her father.

"I think so," he said quietly. "You have only to leave at once, go to a distant city and change your name again. You have no ties, no one…" He saw the girl drop her eyes and impatience touched his tones. "You must not communicate with anyone— anyone at all!"

The girl nodded slowly, "I know, but Paul... won't understand." Paul Shade, she explained, was a clerk in the hotel where she had worked last, where Wentworth had lived. "The one with the curly black hair," she told the Spider seriously. "He's... nice."

"I'll see that he knows you've had to go away," Wentworth assured her, "but you'll have to promise not to communicate with him until I say it's safe."

Beth agreed, then looked up eagerly. "We can go to father, now, can't we? Oh, I'm so worried about him!"

Grimly, Wentworth started the engine of the truck and got it under way. He put Nita and Beth Robertson in the closed body, found the uniform cap he had discarded and donned it. They could not travel far in this truck. It was undoubtedly marked by the police long ago, nor could he seize another car without it being reported. His best chance was to buy a car of some description. His lips tightened at the thought. A further depletion of his small store of funds. It could not be helped.

He knew of a second hand car yard that was open very early and he parked the truck several blocks away, walked there to make his selection. He bought a 1931 Cadillac, produced a set of New Jersey plates which he had stolen from a parked car. It was the best he could do at present. Regardless of how he traveled, he would leave a wide trail. Later in the day, he must buy new plates....

THE PLACE to which Beth's father had fled was not a dozen blocks away and they went there swiftly, labored up long flights of stairs to the fifth floor. At the door, Wentworth silenced his companions, listening tensely. There was no sound from within and he nodded, pressed the bell button in the signal Beth and her father had agreed upon in advance. Through long moments, nothing stirred, then footsteps shuffled across the floor, the door rattled and opened cautiously. Framed in the narrow opening, the face of the old man was gray and wan. There were drawn lines about mouth and eyes, and a strange lack of pleasure at sight of his daughter who ran toward him. He was frightened.

"These people are my friends, father," Beth said eagerly. "They saved me when the men of the Boss tried to kidnap me! Open the door wide, father."

Wentworth saw that the man was not really old, probably in his early fifties. Fear and uncertainty had wrought these lines upon his face and whitened his hair. Wentworth smiled kindly, stepped toward Robertson.

"Let me reassure you," he said pleasantly. "And congratulate you, too. Your daughter is a fine person."

Robertson's face twitched. He stepped back slowly, stiffly, swinging the door wide. Suspicion jerked at Wentworth's heart. The man's actions were so unnatural. As if… as if a gun were held to his back! With a warning cry, Wentworth jerked Nita aside from the door; his automatics leaped to his hands… and he did nothing. From within, a sub-machine gun was leveled at them. Even that would not have stopped Wentworth, but from behind he heard a suave voice he recognized, the voice of the man who had come to collect for the Boss—the Lama of Love.

"So, my friend, you did obey the summons of the Boss!" the man said smoothly. "No, no, do nothing. You are covered by four more of those pleasant little weapons which are so efficient in

61

murder. I refer to sub-machine guns. For yourself, I know, you might brave it, but the ladies... Ah, the ladies!"

Wentworth stiffened, plans of action racing through his brain. The man had put his finger on the difficult point. Whatever he did, Nita and Beth would be sure to fall under the fire of the guns. He turned slowly, heavily, to face the man who spoke so gently. The moon-faced one was not in sight, but the machine gunners he had mentioned were. Their weapons snouted eagerly at Wentworth, at the two women. The faces of the men were determined.

There was no choice left to the Spider. He shrugged. "Very well, I will see this man you call the Boss. To whom do I surrender my guns?"

CHAPTER 6
OBEY—OR DIE!

WENTWORTH'S VOICE was calm, utterly without emotion, but while his brain raced with swift plans, he knew the bitterness of betrayal. It was very plain that the girl had been used to lead him into a trap. That she had been compelled to this action by the fact that they held her father prisoner did not matter. The betrayal remained. Beth Robertson turned to him for help, her eyes appealing. He smiled on her coldly.

For a moment she shrank from his gaze, she held out her hands pleadingly, then she cried out softly in pain. "Oh, no, I didn't," she whispered. "I didn't do that! I wouldn't have led you into a trap. I didn't know they had found my father!"

Wentworth lifted one shoulder in a slight shrug. "It really doesn't matter much what you knew," he said. "The result is the same."

"I think she's telling the truth," Nita put in quietly.

Wentworth nodded. He had said it did not matter, but inwardly it did. He did not see how he could have been so mistaken in the girl. But he had been neatly trapped. Looking back, he could see that the whole thing had been a careful plant. The girl's seizure in the hall outside his room had been deliberate, a reply to his refusal to pay tribute. They had counted on his kindness of heart to cause him to intercede, to follow the thing to its natural conclusion of succoring Beth Robertson's father. And here the Boss' men had waited in utter confidence which, Wentworth realized painfully, had been well justified. He had walked into the trap as neatly as any bungling amateur into police hands!

And he was helpless, as futile against those machine guns as if he were Beth Robertson, to whose eyes tears had risen, who stood brokenly pleading beside him. "It's all right, Beth," he reassured her. "I'm confident you had no conscious part in their plans." He lifted his challenging eyes to the machine gunners. "Well, what are we waiting for?" he demanded.

From his hidden point of vantage, the Lama spoke again, "For the pleasure of the Boss!"

Wentworth detected the faintly metallic timber of the voice, the artificiality which meant it came from a loudspeaker circuit.

Useless to hope that the man would expose himself. Wentworth said nothing further, but stood motionless, waiting. He would match patience with patience. When the Boss understood that be could tantalize the Spider no longer....

It was a full half hour that Wentworth and the two girls stood there. The watchfulness of the machine gunners did not relax. At no time were there fewer than three of the five machine guns trained on him. If there had been only one... Finally the voice of the Lama said softly, "All right."

Curtly, the machine gunners motioned the prisoners into the apartment. Beth's father had collapsed in a chair. Beyond him stood a man whom, despite his mask, Wentworth recognized with a start of surprise he could scarcely conceal. Dodgington, Himman had said, sought to ruin the Spider so as to bring him to judgment before a court. Dodgington had smashed Kirkpatrick and sent him to prison; and now, a dapper small silk mask over his eyes, the man who stood in the apartment to which Wentworth had been summoned to confront the Boss was—*Oscar Dodgington!* There could be no mistaking that thick-chested, stubby body. The dramatic crest of his hair could belong to no other. Even the sweeping fervor of his gestures as he motioned greeting to Wentworth was the same.

Wentworth said dryly, "Why not remove the mask? It really accomplishes very little... Dodgington!"

The prosecuting attorney, for there was no longer any doubt in Wentworth's mind that the man was he, smiled thinly. "Oh, I wish to observe all the formalities," he said lightly. "I'll keep the mask. It is, I believe, in the best super-criminal manner. Won't the ladies be seated?"

NITA MOVED quietly to Wentworth's side and Beth lifted her chin defiantly. Neither spoke. The smile remained on the lips of the masked man.

"If you hesitate to use my name, ladies, and you, Spider, just call me Boss," he said pleasantly. Apparently, he had not recognized Nita, and Wentworth's disguise was still adequate.

Wentworth's hands arched. His guns were in their holsters, for his captors had disdained to take his arms. If this man were the Boss—Wentworth shrugged mentally. No wonder the man had such control over the police as Nita indicated. He knew their innermost secrets. It would be up to him to say which cases were presented to the courts and which were not. By a minute variation in testimony, by failing to present damaging witnesses, or asking them the wrong questions, he could influence the action of grand juries... Wentworth studied the man narrowly. It was fantastic that Dodgington should have turned to crime. But if he had, he would turn one of the most brilliant minds in criminal law to the work. It was patent that he was enjoying the present situation to the full.

When finally he spoke, it was directly to Wentworth. "I sent a collector to receive my share of your last night's enterprise. I understand you refused."

There was a grudging admiration in Wentworth's eyes. The man handled himself so competently. There was no bluster in his manner; his tone was that of polite inquiry.

Wentworth spoke drily, "You are reliably informed."

PRINCESS ISSORIS

YETSE

The Boss nodded. "Just so. I have few failures among my followers. And the failures never fail twice!"

Glancing toward the machine gun men who guarded him, Wentworth saw a grayish pallor creep through their cheeks and

TANG-AKHMUT

DODGINGTON

thought that he fully understood the Boss' remark. But if he were
trying to impress Wentworth, this by-play would not help him.
As if he realized that abruptly, the man spoke in a new tenor.

"Men either obey my commands or die, Spider," he said calmly. "Once more, I ask you for my share of your take."

Wentworth smiled. "Is that a command?"

The Boss' lips curved in an answering smile, but the expression was cold, wolfish. "It is a command!"

"I had an idea it was." Wentworth made no effort to comply with the order. He watched a dark flush creep up the Boss' throat. "Don't you think," Wentworth said carefully, "that all this is a little silly? I am your prisoner, these ladies…" He shrugged. Defiance was foolish under the circumstances. What the Boss wanted was a sop to his ego. He wanted the surrender of what he could easily take. Wentworth wondered idly how long he would live if he reached for his guns. The machine guns fired six hundred rounds a minute, ten a second. Wentworth's tips twitched. Even if he could miraculously accomplish what he wished, the destruction of this man who taunted him, there was more than his own death to contemplate. He had no doubt at all what would be the fate of Nita and Beth whether or not he succeeded in killing the Boss.

"Well?" said the Boss peremptorily.

Deliberately, Wentworth drew a wallet from his hip pocket, crossed to a small table and roughly divided the contents in half. A look of satisfaction crossed the face of the Boss and Wentworth hid his eyes with downcast lids. Let the man think he had won. A reckoning would come. The Spider… Returning to his position, Wentworth stopped rigidly. He realized that, in his mind, he had already rededicated himself to the battle he had abandoned. The Spider would strike again for the freedom of the people, for their release from this criminal overlord who sought to dominate and ruin them! His bitterness at their persecution was still in his breast, but it would not again change his course, or swerve him from his sure destiny. He faced the Boss with a high resolve burgeoning in his heart.

THE BOSS, at the peak of his small triumph, seemed to sense no change in Wentworth. "Thank you," he said gently. "Since you have given me your allegiance, I have an offer to make you."

Hot protest sprang to Wentworth's lips, but he held it down. Was the man such an utter fool… Looking into the cold eyes that peered out through the slits in the mask, Wentworth recognized that the man was far from a fool. The present picture suited his plans somehow.

"I will make you captain of my safecracking squad," the Boss said, with the air of a king conferring a title. "You will train the inept, direct their work, and receive a good percentage of their take. The ladies shall be my hostages for your good behavior!"

Wentworth stared at the man incredulously. Did the Boss really think he would accept such a proffer? Had the Spider, remaining in hiding, lost so much prestige that a criminal thought he could buy him?

The Boss leaned forward, "Come, your promise, Spider. Even we of the Underworld know that you never violate your word of honor." There was mockery in the man, a subtle sneering.

Wentworth laughed. "Let's stop the melodramatics, Dodgington," he said coldly. "You don't for a moment think I'll consider the offer. Let's have the rest of it."

The Boss smiled slightly. "You are refusing my offer? Think

well, Spider! You are a poor man now. The percentage I charged this time was that assessed a member of my organization. To non-members, the fee is ninety percent! I doubt if even you can steal enough to live on ten percent of your take. The offer I make you would provide ample funds. I would not separate you from your love." He bowed mockingly in Nita's direction. "Best hurry before I withdraw the offer."

Wentworth stared at him from under scowling brows. "There can be but one answer," he said quietly. "As you say, I never go back on my word, even to a murdering crook. Consequently, I'll make no pretense of agreeing." He was afire with anger. This man coolly pretended that he had the Underworld under such complete control he could exact the penalties he stated! He thought to intimidate the Spider....

The Boss said, incredulously, "You refuse?"

Wentworth laughed coolly. "Of course."

The Boss shook his head in bewilderment. "Well, every man to his own lunacy. You won't reconsider...."

Wentworth steeled himself to show no emotion when the penalty of refusal was declared upon him. Within him there was a crazy protest. He was dooming Nita and himself for a people who would only cheer when they learned of his death. It was, perhaps, mad, but there was no other course he could take. He was again the Spider and the Spider did not compromise with criminals.

The Boss shrugged in finality. "Very well. Perkins, take them away."

Wentworth braced himself to fight but recognized that

this was not the time. Better to wait… The bald Tibetan came silently from some dark recess of the room, silken yellow robes swishing about ankles cased in scarlet boots. His hairless head shone, his moon face creased in a smile.

"Yes, master," he murmured. "This way, ladies. If you will follow me, sir."

Wentworth whirled to face the Boss again. "Whatever is in store for me," he said harshly, "it is needless to inflict penalties on these two. They are in no way involved in my affairs."

The Boss raised his eyebrows, chuckled. "Really, Spider, you are most ungallant," he said drily. "Do you really wish the ladies to remain my *guests*, while you go free? Yes, that is the penalty that is in store for you. Freedom. Of course, I will expect you to render ninety percent of your future take. That will be all…."

AS HE finished speaking, lights faded out around him so that the corner where he stood was in darkness, while Wentworth was dazzled by brilliant rays. Slowly he moved after the robed lama whom the Boss called by the improbable name of Perkins. Nita and Beth walked stiffly ahead of him and Wentworth heard Robertson being urged to his feet and brought after them. Incredible, the thing that was happening. His offer refused, the Boss was merely turning the Spider loose! But it might be trickery, the execution practiced by Mexicans. A released prisoner shot down in the last possible moment of escape….

The yellow robe of the lama flickered ahead of him down an entire flight of stairs. Wentworth abruptly increased his pace, but when he reached the platform below the man had vanished. He whirled about. Above him, grouped on the stairs, were Nita and Beth and her father, but no one else. The machine gunners had vanished, too!

"Stay an entire floor behind me," Wentworth told Nita. He drew his automatics, made his stealthy way downward. Finally the pavement was reached, the sunlit stretches of the street. Wentworth had forgotten in the dark apartment above that it was day, that outside the sun was shining brilliantly. He paused by the main doors of the apartment while Nita and the others caught up with him.

"What is this trickery?" Nita whispered. "Surely they aren't going to let us go as readily as this?"

Wentworth shook his head. "I don't know," he said. "It may be that the Spider is no longer a man to fear! It may be that the Boss knows me too well and thinks I am good for nothing now but to crack safes."

Nita laughed. "How childish of you, Dick!"

Wentworth grinned, bolted out of the main doors and reached the parked car without hindrance. He made a swift examination to make sure no bomb had been planted in it, then drove back to the apartment where the others waited, and ushered the little party out to the car.

"Circle the block, Nita," he told her. "If I am not back by the third circuit…" He turned and darted back into the building. He could not escape the feeling that there was a trap behind this seeming clemency—or was it contempt?—of the Boss. Swiftly he raced up the steps. At the top floor where before the men of the Boss had awaited him, the apartment door swung open. Wentworth dived through, hit on his shoulders and rolled to his feet, a gun in each hand. No one was in sight. He ran swiftly through the suite and found not only no one in it, but no trace of the men he knew had been here!

Chagrin twisted his face. He bolted toward the door and checked. Was he wrong, or had he heard ghostly laughter somewhere in the far corners of the apartment? But renewed search revealed nothing. He ran through the building, knocking at every door, demanding the right to search. Nita joined him when he reached the third floor and they completed the hunt together. But it was futile. The Boss and his men had vanished, and Wentworth, going to the car, knew bitterly that his release had been absolute. The Boss did not fear the Spider, did not think him even worth killing when he held him a helpless prisoner before the machine guns of his henchmen!

CHAPTER 7
THE LAMA OF LOVE

IF THE Boss had been sincere in his opinion of the Spider, he was sadly underestimating Wentworth's powers. If he had intended his release as a final blow to his morale, already shaken by the public hatred which had been aroused against him, he had overshot the mark. Wentworth's anger, always bitter toward criminals, rose in a furious tide. As he went from the apartment building with Nita, his fists clenched and a whiteness crept into his cheeks. Nita watched him silently. She knew this man of hers so well! When they entered the car, she took the wheel. "Where to?" she asked lightly.

Wentworth's lips moved slightly in a smile that did not lighten the stern lines of his face.

"First," he said quietly, "we must place the Robertsons where they will be safe, then—" His eyes tightened, their depths became cold as ancient ice—"and then, we will pay a call on the Lama of Love!"

If Nita was apprehensive over what lay ahead she gave no outward indication. She drove with deft precision and drew up presently before a quiet hotel. Wentworth gave Beth money.

"I don't think the Boss will bother you again," he told her with a smile that was strangely gentle against the harsh lines of his face. "If he had intended that, he would have kept you prisoner in the apartment. But be careful. If anyone bothers you, or if you have to move unexpectedly, leave me word with that boy at the hotel where we lived. What's his name?"

Beth looked very steadily into his face. "His name is Paul Shade. Do you think it would be dangerous, if I called him, anyway?"

Wentworth assured her it would not, then sprang back to the car. "Dodgington is supposed to be on a fishing expedition up in Maine just now," he told Nita, "so he won't be at his home. If you know where to find my Tibetan lama, get there as rapidly as you can!"

There were little lines of concentration between Nita's troubled eyes as she drove on. A dozen hours ago, she had appealed to Wentworth to bestir himself from his apathy. Now that he was back in the old way again, she was tortured by fears for his safety.

"Do you have any plans, Dick?" she asked him quietly.

Wentworth shook his head slowly. He lounged back at ease and Nita's feeling of strain increased. In the Spider, relaxation meant he was keyed to the ultimate pitch.

"No plans, dear," he replied. "I must find the lama and the man behind him and destroy them." He moved a hand languidly. "The lama in himself is unimportant, an errand boy. But I think that through him… You must remain outside, Nita, and don't think I am doing it to spare you danger! You will be my rear guard!" He tried to make it light, but there was an undertone of gravity in what he said. They both knew well that he was going into deadly danger! The Boss might release him as unimportant when a bullet might have removed him forever, but then he had been a captive. This time he would be an active enemy, invading the stronghold of the Boss! No, they could not fool themselves that so much clemency would be again extended.

A BLOCK from the Temple of Love as the headquarters of the cult was known, Nita pulled to the curb. The building was on Riverside Drive, a private residence that had been successively a millionaire's residence, a girl's school and a lecture hall. Now the cult of the Lama of Love, the minion of the Boss, occupied it. What purpose the cult could serve in the Boss' obviously criminal plans, Wentworth could not fathom. He hoped he might learn that, too, by invasion.

Before the Temple, a long line of luxurious cars waited, each with its uniformed chauffeur. Glancing at them, it was easy to identify the type of people who had thrown themselves into this new cult. Men and women of ordinary circumstances did not drive Rolls Royces or Hispano-Suizas. Wentworth's eyes darkened as he made his way casually up the broad marble steps to the main door of the rich building. As he approached the entrance, the portal swung wide and a Nubian with turbaned head, naked save for baggy trousers of crimson silk, bowed low before him.

"It is necessary that even the initiated wait here," the Negro said in perfect English. "The Lama of Love holds court."

Wentworth played perfectly the part of a slightly skeptical, but nevertheless deeply impressed man. He made the awkward offer of a tip, a bill of large denomination. The Negro refused with fine insolence, stalked across the foyer and placed his shoulders against one of the variegated marble pillars at the foot of a flight of graceful stairs. He folded beautifully muscled arms across his chest and appeared to go into a trance. He was the only guard in sight and Wentworth, after one last glance, let his attention wander.

Drapes of exquisite golden silk cut off rooms to right and left of the main foyer. The ceiling was a dome of inlaid lapis lazuli in which stars of actual gold were scattered. The columns were fluted, slender, draped in silk; in the middle of the foyer a fountain rose and died with such finely adjusted volume that the impact of water falling into water wove a melody of minor notes. Through it, Wentworth could hear a distant chanting, men's voices and women's raised in contrapuntal harmony, and his eyes narrowed as he caught the notes, the archaic words. The language was Coptic. Wentworth knew that, though he could not interpret the words. The hard consonants, the shortened vowel sounds were distinct. And the chant—he could not be mistaken—the chant was the ancient song of the Egyptian Goddess, *Isis!*

Wentworth's lips moved in a faint smile. A Tibetan lama was priest of a degenerate temple of Isis to which wealthy people drove in limousines, and the temple was on Riverside Drive in the heart of the most mechanical capital of the centuries, in New York itself. The thing seemed incredible, but Wentworth had seen too many "impossible" things become reality in the world of crime. The discovery only confirmed his fears that he had a rascal of great ingenuity to fight. Wentworth raised a hand to signal the Negro and when the gesture was ignored, crossed toward him.

Instantly, from the high gallery that circled the azure dome, a man shouted a warning. Glancing that way he continued his progress toward the Negro. Wentworth saw a man in a silken robe of imperial yellow peering down at him. The man held a long-barreled rifle in his hands, the muzzle strangely thickened. With a whispered oath, Wentworth recognized the implement. A silencer! There was no time now for hesitation. It was plain that the man must have recognized him, else the threat of the rifle would not have been so openly exposed. The instant his eyes identified the silencer, Wentworth sprang into action.

A single leap put him beside the Negro. His hands grasped the man's tensed bicep, whirled him about as a shield. He was barely in time. The flat slap of the bullet from the silenced rifle rang through the foyer. The Negro groaned mightily and his body hammered against Wentworth, beaten by the impact of the slug.

WENTWORTH DELIBERATELY fell beneath the Negro. He did not want to use his automatics lest he spread the alarm. He did not want his quarry, the leader, to flee before the hunter even spied it. The silenced rifle spat again and the bullet thudded into the Negro's body. Wentworth let out a pained cry, threshed a little and lay still. From the gallery, the rifleman peered intently for a long moment, then turned away. Immediately, two Negroes brushed aside the curtains of the main room across the foyer, opposite the side from which the murmur of the worshipers came. Their eyes rolled whitely in their black faces as they advanced, but there was no hesitation in their actions. They caught up the dead Negro and Wentworth from the floor, one man to each of them, and crossed swiftly back to the curtains. Wentworth was careful to keep his body wholly inert until the moment came to strike.

Once they were behind the curtains, Wentworth cautiously opened his eyes. He was dumped unceremoniously to the floor and one of the Negroes grabbed a cloth and a bucket from a closet and hurried out. A grimness touched Wentworth's half closed eyes. They were prepared for emergencies, these men, even to the cloth and bucket for washing blood stains from the floor of the foyer! The second Negro dropped on his knees beside the twice-wounded doorman and Wentworth was instantly on his feet. His automatic thudded into his palm and he struck with the same movement that drew it. The Negro crumpled over his companion and Wentworth waited in the folds of the curtain for the return of the other. He was frowning deeply. It seemed likely that one of the yellow-robed priests would come to inspect his kill. He had still a feeling of shock over the grim speed with which the priest had deliberately struck down his own man, because that man was a shield for an enemy!

Minutes dragged past and the third Negro did not return, nor did any of the yellow-robes come to make inspection. Wentworth peered finally through the curtains and saw that the Negro had hidden the pail in the foyer when his task was finished and now stood guard in the same spot where his dead companion had been placed. Wentworth smiled in brief satisfaction. That made it unnecessary for him to delay longer. He bent over the Negro he had knocked unconscious, studied his pulse. He was good for a half hour yet, Wentworth estimated, and without further delay he stole across the room toward a curtained recess which must hide the other exit to the chamber.

Just outside the curtain he paused, listening. He whipped up the drapes and peered beyond. His caution was repaid. A man stood there on guard, a yellow-robed priest! Wentworth sprang back, let the curtain drop, and heard a shrill choked cry from behind it! He waited, gun poised to strike. The curtain stirred quite faintly, then it bellied as something pressed against it from behind and slid slowly downward. Farther and farther out into the room the curtain swayed, then the thing that had disturbed it hit the floor with a crunching thud and the curtain fanned out and spilled its charge, fluttered back to its normal position. The thing that had fallen was a man's body and on the swollen, bald poll crouched a hideous black thing with hairy legs and tiny beady eyes that shone evilly! It was a gigantic spider of some breed unknown to Wentworth and its poisonous fangs were still deep in the poll of the man it had slain.

WITH A shudder of repulsion, Wentworth snatched up a cushion from the floor and crushed the fuzzy thing. Then he stood, his breath coming in slow, deep hissings through his nostrils. He was slowly understanding. The raising and lowering of that curtain was the thing that any person would do on entering the alcove concealed. The priest's cry had come on the heels of that action. Then—then, Wentworth had released that murderous spider and only by good fortune had another fallen instead of himself! Now he was warned. The halls of this temple of love would be studded with death traps for the unwary! Nevertheless, Wentworth must thread them and reach the beast who was behind such monstrosities. There was a way to go through that alcove without releasing the deadly thing that had been set on guard there. But the way would not be discernible to his investigation. Before this, Wentworth had experienced Oriental cunning. It operated with the cruel humor of the East, so that the victim, all unwitting, brought his destruction upon himself.

The death those curtains bore for the unwary might equally have been a poisoned needle that pricked the hand. With a bitter anger, Wentworth gripped the curtains and ripped them from their fastenings. Nothing further happened and he was free to pass through that narrow doorway. He paused to put the ends of the curtain in the hands of the dead priest. Let whoever discovered him think that in his death agony he had torn it down.

Cautiously, Wentworth stepped through the doorway. He saw before him a long, straight hallway whose far end gave on a garden to the rear. On both sides were doorways and, half way along the left wall, a stairway led upward. It had been at the foot of other steps that the Negro had stood guard and Wentworth felt a sudden surety that the man he sought was upstairs.

Nevertheless, he paused at the foot of the steps, searching them closely for some hint of death in their innocent length. He shook his head, grasped the railing—then as quickly released it. A man who had passed that alcove trap would be expected to look for death here. He would be expected to go up those stairs in an unusual way. Smiling thinly, hoping against hope that his touch had not started a hidden mechanism working, Wentworth walked up the stairway, deliberately, in its exact center and without again touching the railing. He reached the top and stood motionless, feeling the high slow thunder of his heart. He dragged his moist palms slowly along his thighs, took an automatic in hand and walked on.

The hallway on the second floor led at right angles to the one below and plainly led to the gallery which the rifleman occupied. There was one other door on the hallway, and Wentworth, after listening there, passed on to that which opened on the gallery. He did not touch the knob, but waited for some sign of life without, for some hint of what next to do. The door was ornate, carved in representation of a huge cornucopia, spilling a multitude of fruits over the entire lower panel. Wentworth was studying the panel attentively when he saw the knob turn. At the same time, two grapes in the design on the panel were depressed. What caught at Wentworth's throat was neither this fact, nor the opening of the door by someone who stood on the farther side. It was what happened when the knob turned. The rim that joined the two halves of the knob together parted and a row of needles, a hundred of them, darted out with the speed of a snake's strike. If Wentworth had grasped and turned that knob, those needles would have pierced his hand through and through! He had no doubt that they were poisoned.

But there was no time to dwell on the narrowness of his escape. The door was opening and a man stepped through, silenced rifle on guard before him. Wentworth struck strongly, seized the priest as he collapsed and drew him to the gallery. He left the door open. Twice, now, he had been saved from death traps. Ultimately, he might have twisted the knob, though the carving of the door had aroused his suspicions. When the Orient uses ornamentation, it usually hides secrets.

IN THE gallery, Wentworth took instant cover behind a column. There were a dozen men and women standing about the fountain foyer. Their voices rose clearly to him, and their chatter was gaily aimless. Too purposeless, it seemed to Wentworth. It was almost as if they sought to hide something behind their casual manner. But he had not time for speculation. He must hurry with his search! If the meeting was breaking up, the lama and his assistant priests, the many singers of the service, would be scattered over the building.

It would be almost impossible then for the Spider to make his tour of investigation without being discovered. Hurriedly, he moved along the circular gallery, keeping close to the wall where the railing interposed between him and those curious eyes below. There was a second door here, ornate as before, and Wentworth hesitated. The East seldom employed the same device twice. What trap guarded this door? He ran back and caught up the body of the unconscious priest, carried it before him. He took the limp hand inside his own like a glove and turned the knob of the door.

Instantly, instead of swinging as an ordinary door, this portal pivoted on a central vertical axis. The floor beneath Wentworth's feet moved with it and in a trice he found himself on the other side of the barrier. Relieved, Wentworth freed the priest, then stepped back, but the body did not fall! It remained oddly erect, the head sagging. And the yellow robe was drenched with blood! With caught breath Wentworth saw that ten keenly pointed blades had telescoped straight out from the door panels! Each of these was fully two feet long and five had penetrated the chest of the priest! They held him as securely erect as if be were nailed to a cross!

Scarcely had Wentworth realized this when he heard a faint hissing noise and pivoted to discover that the wall which he had fancied solid, which made the place in which he stood a narrow corridor, was sliding apart in two sections! The sight they revealed held him momentarily speechless, frozen with amazement. It was like the lifting of a magic curtain, for he was no longer in the heart of New York; he was in an Eastern *seraglio*, the veritable harem of a sultan!

That was his first impression and it clung to him more strongly after he had seen the man who, amid these lolling luxuries of the East, reposed on a draped divan in the middle of this huge and silken room. Women in fluttering slight garments fled behind the curtains, all save one who, before the divan of the man, crouched on her knees. Her dark eyes met Wentworth's steadily, and there was neither fear nor surprise nor any other emotion in their depths.

WENTWORTH TORE his gaze from hers and looked again at the man who had risen to a sitting position on the divan. The face was powerful, lean as a hawk's, with the same predatory cast of features, aquiline nose and gleaming eyes. The mouth was cruelly thin, but above all other things it spoke of strength. He was dressed in a glory of silks; the long, embroidered cloak of the East was spread beneath him; his feet were encased in slippers of scarlet Morocco leather and at his girdle the hilt of a dagger glittered with a dazzling array of precious jewels. These things Wentworth saw in a glance, but it was none of these that held him motionless, that sent a shock as of electricity along his nerves. It was the eyes, great and tawny as any cat's, the will that sat in them like flame. For this was the Man from the East who had ruined Wentworth!

These things Wentworth saw consciously, but above any mere physical vision, he felt the aura of the man. It was evil—evil past any capacity of mere human, evil beyond the scope of human minds; evil with an ancient horror that reached back through the centuries to the days when Egypt quivered under the lash of the Pharaohs, when Babylon and Nineveh were scarlet. Wentworth would have sworn he had learned these things and yet the man had not moved!

Wentworth knew in that instant, he *knew* that from this man stemmed all the crime and bloodshed that had been heaped upon the city! With no more testimony than this fugitive glimpse, the Spider judged this man and found him guilty. His ready gun leaped to his hand and he leveled it at the breast of the Oriental on the divan.

"Death!" Wentworth cried, and the harshness of his intonation rasped on his ears. "Death to thee, thou root of all evil!" Even the words were strange and unnatural, strange that he should so address this man upon whom he had never laid eyes before, whom he had never suspected existed. He shook his head to drive the uncertainty from his brain. The man was evil, but there was no man who could be evil with a bullet through his heart. The Spider's gun would resolve all difficulties. His finger closed down on the trigger!

CHAPTER 8
BLOODLESS DEATH

I N THE act of firing the shot that would kill the man and eliminate all the turmoil of crime that had been loosed in the city, Wentworth found that his gun was centered on an entirely different target. From her crouching position before the divan, the girl had risen and calmly interposed her body between the gun and the Man from the East!

Furiously, Wentworth thrust her aside. The girl subsided on the floor with a little whimper of hurt while her eyes still implored him. Triumph swelling his heart, Wentworth jerked up his gun again and—his eyes met those of the Man!

Once more the tingling as of an electric shock raced through his body. The Man's tawny cat's eyes seemed to grow enormous, to march toward him like swelling lakes. And Wentworth's gun was as useless as a stick! Through the Man's eyes, from their depths, spoke the white-hot thing that was the will of this anciently evil being.

"You are but a man," Wentworth felt rather than heard the words, and they beat upon his brain with a force like bullets. "You are but a man and no man can prevail against the godhead! Thy will is a potent thing but beside the will of the godhead it is as a bent reed beside the stout body of an oak. Thy will does not even wish to offend mine. Thy will is eager to serve."

Wentworth's lips shrank back from his teeth, his eyes widened under the assault of the man's naked will. Wentworth had fought hypnotism before and though he knew that he had never before met such a will as this, he did not yield. He would not yield! He had long ago learned how such hypnotism must be combated.

He must concentrate on one simple thing and let nothing swerve him from the contemplation of that thing. It must not be something on which his eyes gazed, lest his vision become wearied and help to betray his mind. He concentrated on pulling the trigger of the automatic. Every nerve, every muscle in his body, pointed toward that one thing—the mere tightening of his finger which would serve to pull the trigger. He forgot the cat eyes that burned into his and the forgetfulness reduced their size until they ceased to be lakes of menace and became

mere eyes again. Hateful, glaring eyes,
but nevertheless a human man's eyes.
WENTWORTH'S HEAD
bowed a little, his shoulders hunched
with the effort to tighten that first
finger which rested on the trigger of
his gun; his legs bent with the strug-
gle and sweat sprang out on his fore-
head. Thoughts continued to pour unhindered into his brain,
but they were not so complex now. They had descended to the
ancient, simple formula: "My will above thine, O human! *My
will above thine!*"

Wentworth did not contend with that statement. He willed
his muscles, his nerves, to do just one simple thing to tighten
his finger on the trigger. But, strive as he might, he could not
fire the gun!

He knew that his respite was drawing to a close. Soon the
lama would enter the door behind him, the door on whose spikes
dangled the body of another priest. And in that instant, if Wentworth had not won this contest of wills, he would die! Wentworth heard a fierce panting and knew that it was the laboring
of his own breath. He was aware of perspiration stinging in his
eyes; but the man on the divan was laboring, too. He sat bolt
upright, trying to breathe in the deep, natural rhythm which
strengthens the body for trial. His forehead was dappled with
sweat, his upper lip and the soft places beneath his eyes were
beaded. He didn't move, but his eyes fought for him. There was

no doubt now that this was indeed the Man Wentworth sought, the criminal intellect….

Wentworth heard in his mind footsteps his ears could not detect, the hurrying footsteps of the lama; and in the lama's hand was a long, keen sacrificial knife. A bewilderment touched Wentworth. How could he hear and see those things? And with the doubt came triumph. He heard and saw the things because the Man had put the thoughts into his brain to distract him! He hoped by these things to crack the concentration which was Wentworth's armor.

At the thought, strength seemed to thrill through Wentworth's every vein. Laughter, ugly, angry stuff, poured from his lips. With an effort that seemed to crack the fibers of his brain, he tugged the trigger of the automatic. The explosion was the crack of doom. It wrenched the automatic from Wentworth's hand and, feeling the burst of fire in his brain, he realized what had happened. Unable to crack the will that held a finger to the trigger, the man had worked subtly on Wentworth's brain. The man had caused the Spider to bend his wrist before he fired the shot, so that the bullet had been directed, not at the enemy, but at himself!

If the strategy had failed, it was not because it lacked cleverness, but because the man who locked wills with the Spider lacked the strength to finish the maneuver. As it was, he thought Wentworth dead and the power of that thought and fits own exhaustion hurled Wentworth to the floor in a swoon that was brother to death!

IT WAS at that instant the lama burst in. Still, through the close rapport Wentworth held with the will of the man on the divan, he could feel the tardy entrance of the priest, feel the anger of the man who received him.

"No, you will not use the knife of sacrifice upon him," came the Man's rich, deep voice. "He is a better and a greater man than you, Yetse. Never have we met a stronger will, and we have dueled with the lord and master of all will and all life!"

And the Tibetan lama, whom Dodgington had called Perkins and whom this man called by the strange name of Yetse, bowed low.

"As the Pharaoh orders," he whispered, "as is the will of the mighty, the immortal Tang-akhmut...."

Darkness claimed Wentworth wholly then, but not the darkness caused by any wound. The bullet had missed him cleanly. Through the darkness, he felt strange things. He saw nothing, he heard nothing, but over and over in his brain he felt the presence known as the Pharaoh, Tang-akhmut. Gradually that impression faded from him and he had only a sensation of great peace, of warmth and security; of love.

It was with a reeling dizziness of delight that Wentworth finally regained his senses. He opened his eyes slowly and gazed up at a ceiling draped in cerulean silks. Silk was against his body and beside him was the warmth of another being. He turned his head languidly and the madness of a woman's hair tingled across his mouth. He started up, staring at the sleeping woman beside him, at the relaxed face of the girl who had tried to prevent him from killing Tang-akhmut, who called himself Pharaoh. A shudder swept over Wentworth. In Heaven's name, what had happened in that swoon? He sprang to his feet and the woman stirred and opened her eyes. She smiled, rose to her knees and grace-fully bowed her forehead to the floor.

"Master," she whispered.

Wentworth bent and twined his fingers in her hair, pulled her to her feet. "Who are you?" he demanded harshly, "and how do you come to be here beside me?"

The woman's lips still smiled. "I am thy slave, master, and where would a slave be but at her master's side?"

Impotent fury rose in

The rope was fastened not to his wrists but to his thumbs.

Wentworth. He released his hold on her and strode across the cushioned floor of the room, suddenly aware then that his normal clothing had been stripped from him and that he wore the silken robes of the Orient! He spun back to the woman.

"Your name?" he demanded.

She shook her head and her answer came in a singsong that crackled in Wentworth's senses, "I have no name save love!"

He nodded sharply. That was it. The woman was hypnotized! Her answers had been embedded in her subconscious. He asked her quickly a few more questions and listened acutely to the replies. Yes, he had been right Hypnotism. Wentworth drew her tenderly to her feet. Only one person could rouse her, the one who held her in thrall, but it was plain that she had been instructed to obey the Spider!

"I bid my slave to sleep," Wentworth said gently.

The girl's dark eyes closed and she sagged against him.

Wentworth lowered her to the cushions and covered her with silks. He stood over her for a moment, pity in his eyes. God alone knew who this lovely child was, or what her fate— God and Tang-akhmut! Anger chilled Wentworth's gaze. He plunged from the room and found himself in a hallway that, like the place he had quitted, was draped in silk. The air was heavy with perfume. Wentworth wrenched at the embroidered stole about his throat.

Strangely, he had no thought of death as he strode through the hallway. Traps there had been in plenty at the entrances to this cushioned hell, but within? These were the quarters of the harem. They would not be… He swept aside a soft drape, stepped into a large chamber through whose ceiling slanted the silk-strained rays of the sun. The chamber was empty save for one woman who turned toward him as he entered. She wore no harem garb, but a long robe of heavy white silk that clasped over one shoulder with a golden bauble and left the other warmly bare. Her hair was ruddy gold. She stared at him curiously, unafraid, unmoving.

WENTWORTH STRODE directly toward her and as he advanced he felt anger stir within him. For here, modeled softly in curves, was the same face that graced Tang-akhmut and in these tawny eyes was the same bitter power of the Pharaoh's gaze! Kinswoman of the Pharaoh....

Wentworth stopped and realized he had spoken the words aloud. This was madness, a pipe-dream beyond the realm of possibility. They had drugged him with opium and hashish....

"Who are you," the woman demanded, her voice imperious, "that you enter our chambers and speak to us thus familiarly? It is true that we are the sister of the Pharaoh, Princess Issoris."

Wentworth moved on slowly, his eyes veiled under heavy lids, his mouth not smiling, but hard and unrelenting. For a moment the girl shrank from his stern regard, then she laughed softly. Her eyes were veiled, too.

"You are a curious man, and fear is not in you," the woman who called herself Issoris said. "Do you know that our brother would strangle you with his own hands if he found you here?"

Wentworth was within arm's length of Issoris and she did not draw away. Her arms hung placidly at her sides, her tips were smiling, and there was a quick lift to the rounded breasts that the draped robe half revealed.

"Do you know," she said softly, "that we half believe we like you, bold stranger?"

Wentworth stood and looked on her. "You know your brother's secrets," he said. "You hold Yetse and the others in the palm of your hand."

The girl bent her head in assent. "What you say is true," she said. "All these things, these powers, we could give… to the man we love!"

She swayed toward him, arms half lifting, but Wentworth stood motionless, watched her narrowly. Had Tang-akhmut hypnotized his sister also into a submissive harem woman? The thought was dismissed at once from his mind. There was a deeper game than that here. Perhaps, Issoris was renewing the offer made to him by the masked man who so resembled Dodgington; if it were not for the actual physical resemblance to Tang-akhmut, Wentworth felt that she might easily have been planted here merely to inveigle submission from the Spider!

He had to think swiftly. He was in the midst of some stronghold of Tang-akhmut, whether the Temple of Love he did not know. Certainly the exits would be guarded by the awful traps he had so narrowly escaped, and others which he would be less likely to avoid. Even to reach Tang-akhmut again might be beyond his capacity. But with this woman's help… He studied her face again and was convinced. She was what she claimed to be, the sister of that sinister Man. Through her he might reach and slay Tang-akhmut He might gain escape for himself and the poor slaves here.

GIRDING HIMSELF with that thought, Wentworth moved slowly toward Issoris. He swept the sister of Tang-akhmut into his arms! Issoris' eyes closed under his kiss. He felt the primitive and fierce surrender of her body, then she leaned back and opened her eyes widely to gaze into his.

They were her brother's eyes and his will gazed through them, his will and his evil soul! It was not mere abandon Wentworth saw there. That, Wentworth would have been prepared for. It was the stark cruelty of a cat, the soulless selfishness of a savage queen. It was ancient and her evilness plumbed depths to which no sane man could set a name. There was cold and acid poison eating at her soul—and it would destroy him!

All Wentworth's powerful will, all his desire to serve humanity, could not drive him on just then. Revulsion seized upon him. He started up from her embrace and, despite his iron control, the hatred of her writhed in his eyes.

For one tense moment they crouched like that, the woman on the floor with her lifted, eager arms, the man on his knees, hands thrusting away in the revulsion of the soul which he could not restrain. Then Issoris bounded up like a lithe cat and threw her robe about her. She shouted fierce sounds in the guttural tongue of Yetse and, in brief seconds, a half dozen of the scarlet-pantalooned Negroes bounded into her chamber! Bulbous eunuchs they were, but there were six of them. They fell upon Wentworth, wrenched his arms behind his back and then hung him dangling from a ceiling beam.

Over the heads of the Negroes who, he knew, were preparing to torture him, he gazed into the eyes of Issoris and the cruelty he had detected glowed fiercely there. She could not remain in one spot, but, fiercely as a waiting cat, she crouched back and forth across the room, her lithe body plain beneath the heavy folds of silk. If it had been love that stirred her, its place was taken now by sold hatred… The Negroes were stripping the clothing from Wentworth's body and presently one of them darted away to return moments later with an armful of thin rubber wands. For a moment, after each of the Negroes had taken a wand, there was silence in the draped room. Issoris moved close to Wentworth, put her arms about his neck, her body against his. She laughed into his face and her small white teeth were like a cat's.

"You shall learn, bold stranger," she whispered, "of the love of Issoris!"

She bit his cheek and, though the blood flowed, he did not wince. Issoris stepped back and cried a harsh command. The Negroes, with their delicate rubber wands, began to beat Wentworth over his entire body!

THEY DID not strike hard. No one blow was actually painful, but Wentworth knew what would follow. He was dangling from his arms, wrenched about behind him, and that in itself was a refined torture in the Middle Ages. Issoris had introduced an improvement. The rope that suspended him was fastened not to his wrists, but to his thumbs!

And the thin wands of rubber tap-tapped over his body. The sultans had devised the *bastinado*, the beating that was inflicted upon the soles of the feet with a light rod of bamboo. But it was not a beating so much as a tapping. And after a while the skin of the soles became swollen and as the tapping continued it blistered and burst. If the tapping stopped then, the man might walk again some day, but often it did not stop there. Wentworth knew that this *bastinado* of his entire body would not cease until insanity released him from its pain! The Negroes knew how to strike and where; already the sensitive skin was beginning to swell. Wentworth clamped his teeth upon his lower lip. There would be no surcease, no help. A woman scorned....

In the midst of the agony that racked him, Wentworth's thoughts grew disconnected. He could cling to only one idea. He must not give this woman the satisfaction of a single moan of pain. Issoris was motionless now. She stood apart and her eyes glowed. From the corner of her slim mouth a thread of blood was scarlet against her white skin....

The impact of his fall to the floor roused Wentworth from a stupor of pain. He thrust himself weakly up, intent still on defiance, and he heard a cry of pain that was not his own. He became aware of the Negroes crouched to the floor around him, of a flailing whip. And then he saw Tang-akhmut. There was something terrible about the man in that moment!

Wentworth's vision wavered and re-focused and he heard again the cry and recognized the voice of Issoris. When he could see clearly, he realized that she had been swung aloft by her wrists to the same beam which had held him. He saw Tang-akhmut rip the clothing from her white body, saw him step back and swing a long limber whip savagely across her hack....

Issoris' white, tortured body was the last distorted vision Wentworth held as he sank into the depths of unconsciousness. He was in darkness for a long while and the slave girl came and tended to him. He lost count of time. Night and day were indistinguishable. He gathered his strength. Once in every twenty-four hours, Tang-akhmut came to talk to him. Always, there was the battle of the wills. Of Issoris he made no mention.

The Pharaoh invariably laughed when it was finished. "Does your will grow weak or strong, O Spider?" he demanded.

Wentworth smiled at him slightly,—a stiff movement of hard lips. "It remains strong, Tang-akhmut," he said coldly. "It is still strong enough to overcome yours!"

For a moment anger flared redly in the Egyptian's eyes, then he laughed. "Yes, yours is the stronger," he said ironically. "That is why I am a prisoner here and you are the lord!" He rose gracefully to his feet. "But you have a mighty will. Tonight, I shall test it fully. We have some prisoners and I have designed certain entertainment for them." The way he pronounced the words sent cold chills over Wentworth's body. He could guess what the certain entertainments would be.

"Beside my methods," Tang-akhmut went on fondly, "those of my sister are somewhat antiquated. But you shall see for yourself! Rest well, my adversary."

Scarcely had Tang-akhmut vanished when the curtain whipped aside and Wentworth gazed up into the tawny eyes of Issoris. She carried in her hands one of the thin rubber wands, but her lips held a smile, her burning golden hair swung silken over her shoulders. Strangely, she dropped on her knees beside Wentworth!

"My master," she whispered, and still she seemed more dream-like than real. "If thou wilt but pay my price, thou shalt go free this night, and later—" she drew in a deep breath—"thou shalt learn all the secrets your brain can contain!"

Wentworth rose unsteadily to his feet. Physically, he was still weak and the battle of wills with Tang-akhmut had been exhausting. But this was no dream. Issoris offered him freedom!

"The price?" Wentworth demanded harshly.

The woman gazed up at him with her cat eyes and her mouth parted in a slow smile. Wentworth grated out a curse. He snatched the rubber wand from her and struck her. Issoris laughed richly. She crawled toward him.

Wentworth hurled the rubber wand to the floor. "Lead me out of here," he said savagely, "and any price you can ask will be too little!"

CHAPTER 9
THE AVATAR OF SEKHMET

ISSORIS REMAINED on her knees before him and slowly he regained calmness. Her golden head was bowed almost worshipfully, her slim hands, with their nails tinted with antimony, were clasped against her breasts. Over a robe of simple white she wore a long gray cloak which included a cowl to cover her head. Belatedly, Wentworth remembered that he had no weapons, that in the clothing he wore, he could not even travel the streets of New York. He was penniless.

Roughly, he pointed out these things to Issoris and she promised that he would be provided with what he needed before he left. She rose to her feet, exquisitely graceful. When her eyes were not upon him, Wentworth could almost feel pity for this gracious creature. He remembered that the whip of Tang-akhmut had cut into her white flesh.

"Before I leave," he said thickly, "I must meet Tang-akhmut again!"

As if she read his thoughts, Issoris moved close to him. "Fear not," she said softly, "in your escape you will avenge me on my brother. Someday, you two shall meet and you shall not walk away from that meeting vanquished! I know… I feel the future hot within me!"

For a moment more she stood close beside Wentworth, then she moved to the curtained exit of the room and, reaching through, brought back such a robe as she herself wore, Wentworth drew this on over his silken clothing, pulled up the cowl.

"Tonight," Issoris whispered, "the devotees of Sekhmet gather in the caverns beneath the Temple! There is a new avatar and there will be many robed as we are moving through the passages. We will be safe among them. When we have reached the Temple of Bast…" There was a glow in Issoris' eyes that was like the eyes of the cat-headed goddess she named. A coldness touched Wentworth. He did not trust Issoris, yet no other course than the one she offered was open to him.

"Lead on!" he said harshly.

Like gray ghosts, they glided together through corridors and chambers that were at first silk-draped and deeply cushioned. Presently, this gave way to stone flooring and somber walls of rock that were lit only by the occasional yellow pools of flaring torches. Still the sweet and heavy perfume of the Temple of Love went with them. They moved among many other figures clad as they were, Wentworth saw. The others converged from side passageways, they slippered ahead of him, came behind. He was hemmed in by scores of gray ghosts moving in a strange silence. Uneasiness crept into Wentworth's brain. What guarantee did he have that this woman did not plan treachery. She spoke of a new avatar of Sekhmet. Might she not mean that he himself….

He thrust the idea aside. Sekhmet, of ancient Memphis, was the lion-headed goddess of war and destruction but, with the cunning of the Egyptian priesthood, she had been served by women. The Temple of Bast, Issoris had called this cavern to which they moved. But Bast was only another name for the dread Sekhmet. In the delta of the Nile, they had turned her lion's head into that of a cat, and they had given her the symbols and the graceful body of a dancing girl. This was the goddess, Bast… But there had been many queer perversions of the Egyptian gods and goddesses, altered to suit the political needs of the priests, to match the current degeneracy of the people about them. Thus Isis, who had been a wholesome goddess of the crops, a Mother Nature with a child upon her knee, had become latterly a goddess of fecundity, or propagation, and then degenerated into a debased Venus of passion and sensuality. And in this cavern beneath the multifarious New York, what hideous form might not Sekhmet the Awful take?

WENTWORTH'S THOUGHTS flowed fluidly through his brain, returned again to the mention of the avatar of Sekhmet. Too often, in the fiercer days, the avatar had been no more than a mock-holy sacrifice… He thrust such memories from his brain, sent his glance sideways to the bowed face of Issoris. Her eyes glided to meet his and the thin pale line of her lips stirred. Was he mistaken, or was there mockery in that smile!

"How much farther?" he asked with lip-movements alone.

Issoris shook her head gently, nodded ahead, seeming to say only a short distance. But she did not speak and her manner indicated that silence would be the test part. Yet, surely, all these about him were not of her race. There must be here many of those whose rich motors he had seen—how long ago?— parked before the Temple of Love. Many times his thoughts had swung to Nita, waiting in the car for his return. Had she made a rash entrance into the temple? But, no. If she had been made a captive, if anything of that sort had occurred, he would surely have been taunted with the knowledge. Tang-akhmut would have gloated over watching the play of expression on his prisoner's face, over the effect upon his morale….

Ahead, the corridor took an abrupt turn and a vast chamber opened up before Wentworth. The columns of living rock had been polished and engraved with the hieroglyphs of ancient Egypt, and Wentworth was stunned with the thought of the hours of labor represented in this crypt beneath the teeming city of New York. In God's name, how long had this horror festered? How long had Tang-akhmut planned and waited for the moment to strike down those who might stand in his path?

His eyes searched the corridors among the columns and everywhere that the gray-clad multitude was assembled. Issoris touched his arm and led him straight forward through the Temple of Bast toward what, he realized, must be the altar itself. As they advanced, a greenish fight waxed on the margin of his vision, strengthened and became a flood. He stopped in his tracks, Issoris' hand on his arm dragged him to his knees, and he realized that all about him the gray cowled figures had kneeled also. For he was gazing upon the fearsome statue of Sekhmet, the Lion-headed, the Awful, Goddess of War and Destruction—Goddess of Crime and Murder, Wentworth realized suddenly. That was the role for which that ancient cruel idol had been cast in New York.

Beneath the edge of his cowl, he studied the great crouching figure and from behind the throne on which Sekhmet sat issued long, silent files of dancing girls. Their clothing was the stiff, archaic skirt of ancient Egypt, more transparent than any silk. Their young breasts were bared except for the circular wide collar of many colors which hung from their throats.

They began to whirl, to posture with fluid grace, through a ritual dance. But no such dance as this had ever been enacted in ancient Memphis. Its evil was a subtle thing, its debased obscenity something to turn the stomach of a normal being. Wentworth's head whirled, but he watched—watched as the lines of dancing girls formed and reformed, as the posturing grew wilder, more frantic. Cymbals clashed and a drum with

103

a muted head made eccentric but monotonous rhythms. There was a thin, nasal piping and none of the musicians was visible.

Distantly, a chanting began, women's voices blending together so that they seemed not many voices, but one voice of great volume and many tones. A darkness gathered about the throne of Sekhmet and a start tugged at Wentworth's muscles, his breath caught in his throat. The eyes of Sekhmet glowed crimson with the flickering, changing gleam of… of fire! When he looked back to the dancing girls they had vanished. The chanting grew louder, and from the dark mouth of a cavern off to the left the flickering small lights of many candles began to show. They shed little light, illumined no more than the faces of those who carried them, and those faces were all tilted upward, chanting. IN ALL that mass of priestesses, there was no touch of color. They, too, wore the uniform gray of the worshippers and Wentworth felt that lack as a deliberate thing. He could not have said how the feeling came to him, but it was there, and he knew that soon that monotony of color would he broken; this deep monody of melody broken… His eyes flicked back to Sekhmet and a curse started from his throat. He held it back, watching narrowly. The light was stronger on the statue and he could make out certain features more clearly. The head of the goddess bent forward slightly, and the arms were pivoted at the shoulders! Behind those strange, bestial eyes, the flickering red light grew.

Issoris bent close to him, apparently sensing his restlessness. "We dare not leave before the service is finished," she said softly. "When there are scores of people leaving, you can easily mingle with the departing crowds. I will tell you what you need to know, and…" She stopped then, and Wentworth wordlessly cursed the lack of control which had permitted her to feel the jerk of a start. For the ranks of gray had parted and forth from that colorless mass, six nearly naked men staggered forward. Their hair hung long and stiff, square-cut to their shoulders, and about their throats and loins were the circular, many-colored bands which Egyptian slaves had anciently worn. But it was not at these that Wentworth gazed. These men bore on their shoulders a flower-decked litter and on it reposed a woman clad in blood-scarlet robes!

Issoris laughed. "The avatar!" she whispered.

The avatar, decked in garlands of flowers like a sacrificial offering, had her face turned toward the awful face of Sekhmet, but a sense of familiarity, of pain, stabbed through Wentworth's heart. All about him was the groaning murmur of the gray-clad hosts as they saw the avatar in scarlet. It was cleverly done, that scarlet, striking the woman out clearly amid all the gray monotony. But it was not that which pulled Wentworth far forward on his knees, straining against the hand of Issoris.

In the background had appeared a gaunt, powerful man who wore a mask like the goddess' lion face. He stood with arms folded across his powerful chest and the litter was lowered to the steps of the dais before him. The avatar in scarlet rose slowly to her feet, stepped from the litter and faced out toward the assembled throng. Her bare, exquisite arms lifted and Wentworth surged irresistibly to his feet.

For this lovely woman, this avatar of Sekhmet clad for the sacrifice was… God, it couldn't be, and yet… No, he couldn't be mistaken. Every line of that graceful body, every curve of that beloved face, he knew. The avatar was… Nita van Sloan!

Desperately, Wentworth flung his glance about him. As yet he had no idea what form the worship of Sekhmet would take. It might merely be some harmless hocus-pocus in which Nita must participate. So he counseled himself, but he knew, he *knew* that it was more than that. Death and degradation were here… Luckily, many of the gray-clad worshippers had surged to their feet with him. He was aware of Issoris close beside him, her eyes fixedly on his face. And now he was certain of the mockery there!

Damn the woman out of hell, she had known that Nita van Sloan was precious to him. Somehow, she had penetrated that fact. Or perhaps she had only guessed at some connection between this captive who must surely have been taken on the same day on which he himself had invaded the stronghold of Tang-akhmut. And her mercy, her rescue of him from the toils of the Pharaoh was mere pretense to bring him here! There must be guards in these gray robes around faun, armed men placed to prevent him from hampering whatever hellishness was to be enacted there upon the altar.

NITA'S VOICE rose clearly high above the monotony of the chanting, weaving a furiously mounting theme. The litter was gone, but in the shadows about the knees of Sekhmet the men still waited, strong arms folded on their chests. Wentworth tried to catch Nita's eye, but her rapt gaze was fixed and a sense of overwhelming defeat, or bitter rage, swept over Wentworth. She had been hypnotized. She would follow out faithfully the orders given to her subconscious mind by her "control," even if that order meant fantastic death on the knees of that grim goddess of terror!

"When this fool woman has sacrificed herself," said Issoris softly, "you shall escape. I promise you a meeting with my brother in which you shall be on equal terms! Unless you meet and overpower him, he and his killing, his robberies will lay waste the entire city! Nothing can stop him—nothing but you!"

Wentworth's lips twisted. He realized what Issoris was doing to him, as if he had not already shouted that fact to the will which bade him leap forward and battle to the death to save Nita! Well she knew the ideal of the Spider's service which put that service above all other things, even his own life and that of his loved ones. If he would permit Nita to act out the last detail of her self-sacrifice, he could go free to strike at Tang-akhmut! He thought, probably, that this time she spoke truth—that her admiration of a man who could withstand such mental torture would be so great, she would help him with freedom. Tang-akhmut....

Wentworth forced his lips to a frigid smile. "I do not enjoy such scenes as this. I could wish the avatar would hurry with her foolishness. I must escape—quickly!"

While he spoke, his veiled eyes cast about him. He was without a weapon. Issoris doubtless carried nothing but a dagger, if that. But the guards, they would have some deadly thing, swords or... If only one of them carried a gun! They were not above modern weapons, as witness the attack upon himself with a silenced rifle.

Of the closest figure, he took swift account. He kept the smile on his lips, but his eyes became more deeply veiled. He was fifty feet from the altar where Nita, with lifted arms, drew her wailing song of sacrifice to a close. A surprise attack… He doubted if any save those closest to him were guarding him. Those others… If he rushed toward the altar crying out some nonsense about Sekhmet, probably they would let him pass.

As if Issoris guessed something of his purpose, her two hands closed tightly on his left arm, her body dragged against him. Her voice was a passionate sound without meaning. On the altar, Nita turned with majestic stride, her proud little head held high, and walked toward the figure of the goddess Sekhmet. With no more preliminary than that, she flung herself into the arms that rested upon the figure's knee—and those arms began to lift!

Now, Wentworth knew the meaning of that fire-light dance behind the eyes of Sekhmet. For the lion's mouth opened and from that awful maw, little pantings of flames began to spew. The tongues of flame licked longer and longer toward Nita's supine body. And the arms, clamping her precious form tightly, were lifting Nita inexorably into those flames that pushed their murderous heat out between the jaws of Sekhmet!

It had come sooner, more swiftly, than Wentworth could possibly have imagined. Within another few seconds, those flapping, devouring flames would scorch Nita's breast, would consume her flesh slowly while she writhed in anguish, unable to escape the mechanical embrace of the arms of Sekhmet! Soundlessly, Wentworth threw his free arm about Issoris. He lifted her clear of the floor and with the same movement hurled her bodily against the nearest guard.

"Nita!" he shouted. "Nita, save yourself! The Spider commands it!"

AS HE cried the warning aloud, he sprang with all his weight upon the shoulders of the man before him, clamped a strangling forearm about his throat. Their gray robes bellied and flapped about them and the gathering guards could not tell which was friend and which foe. Deliberately, Wentworth allowed the man to continue his struggles while his free hand flew over his body to find whatever weapon he carried. A gasp of thankfulness sobbed from Wentworth's throat. A revolver!

He ripped the weapon clear of its sheath, sprang from the subsiding figure of the strangled guard and charged toward the altar.

"Nita, Nita!" he cried. "Save yourself from Sekhmet!" On the arms of Sekhmet, Nita cried out in sharp pain, stirred, and stared about her in a daze. The flames had touched her, and the hypnosis fell from her like a cloak.

"Save yourself!" Wentworth shouted.

He saw Nita struggle against the clamp of the mechanical arms that held her, saw that she could scarcely move. God, there was no hope there and, grouping about the throne of Sekhmet, the six men who had borne the avatar's litter waited for him, waited with grinning mouths and keen knives that thirsted! Behind them, Wentworth's eyes sought out one man who did not join in the defense, but who gripped a lever at which he tugged with straining arms. A shout of rage rasped in Wentworth's throat. The gun in his hand spoke and the man was hurled from the lever by the impact of lead.

Now another figure entered the battle. Stately and dignified as upon the altar, the man with the cat's-head mask seized the lever and Wentworth's second shot had no more effect on him than if he had been an effigy made of stone. Wentworth deduced armor, but he could not know what place that bullet-proof sheathing ended. There was no time. His shots to save Nita had brought him almost to the foot of the throne of Sekhmet and the knifemen who defended it waited no longer. With cries like beasts of prey, they sprang to the attack!

Wentworth became a madman. His gun blasted again and he dodged a thrown knife that he scarcely saw in the gloom of the temple. He whirled then and ran a swift ten feet from the throne, leveled his revolver and emptied its three final shots in a swift drum roll. Not at the knifemen who even now were charging to the attack again, but at the grotesque image of Sekhmet! It was not the madness it seemed. His lead sped true at the target he had selected. The heavy slugs of forty-five caliber lead, beating upon the statue with the impact of a quarter ton in foot-pounds, might do what his puny strength and Nita's struggles could not avail!

THE FIRST shot smashed squarely into the slot of the statue's shoulder directly at the pivot. Flame gushed from the wound like leaping blood and it became apparent that the entire interior of the figure of Sekhmet was filled with fire. Wentworth glimpsed this fragmentarily and battered the second bullet on the heels of the first Wentworth knew from the sound of his lead hammering against that shoulder, driving it away from the body, that it was not steel. And against anything else, yes, even stone, his lead might do its work. He hesitated a moment before that last shot. The knifemen were almost upon him. Wentworth shouted, leaped to the altar and flung his last bullet squarely into the notch his other shots had dug. The arms of Sekhmet faltered, shivered. Nita screamed, wrenched violently and—the left arm of Sekhmet slipped from its pivot and thudded to the floor, smashed to fragments. Nita slithered from the grip of the remaining hand, fell upon the idol's knees and clung there, fainting... And the knifemen closed in upon Wentworth, in whose hands was only an empty gun!

Wentworth threw back his head and shouted his defiant laughter into their faces. The temple was in chaos. The priestesses had fled; gray-clad worshippers were dashing to and fro madly without purpose and against that stream a few of the guards struggled forward. Frantically, Wentworth's eyes quested about him. And then Wentworth saw the thing he looked for, a narrow platform up there near the vault of the Temple, and, dangling from it, a rope ladder. This was the ultimate guard of the priests of Sekhmet. From that point, they would defend themselves if all other means failed. But this time they had been overconfident, trusting too much in the close guards about Wentworth, trusting too much in Issoris. With a shout, Wentworth flung his empty gun into the face of the nearest man, went over his head in a lunging dive and seized that dangling rope ladder—with his hands. The momentum of his leap swung him out over the heads of the attackers, though knives reached for him. Squarely on the knees of Sekhmet, Wentworth leaped. With a derisive cry, he whirled to snatch up Nita's fainting body—and his cry went flat in his throat, became thwarted hope and despair. For Nita was gone—and gone also was the cat-headed man in armor!

CHAPTER 10
EMPTY VICTORY

WENTWORTH'S DISCOVERY struck him with a sense of irreparable loss. He was stunned, stricken in the moment of victory. But there could be no delay, there must be none. The men of Tang-akhmut were closing in on him from all sides. The worshippers were his enemies, howling for his death. Wentworth sent a single piercing scrutiny over the cavern temple. There were many exits but the crowd blocked them all. Not that way could the cat-headed one have fled with Nita.

Wentworth sprang from the knees of Sekhmet toward the dark gloom that clustered thickly behind her. From behind here somewhere the dancing girls had come and had retreated. There must be an opening—Blackly he saw it, an inky spot on a black wall. It was narrow, a slit more than a doorway. In long bounds, Wentworth reached the spot and dived through. Something fanned his back with a gust of air. There was a rending, crunching concussion that drove him to his knees. For a moment he swayed there, dazed, then he reeled to his feet, groped back of him to discover the reason for that sound. He knew already that all sound, all light from the temple, had been shut out in the same instant....

He felt behind him and, uncontrollably, a shudder jerked at his muscles. A block of stone fully ten feet in thickness, a block which filled the passageway from roof to floor, from wall to wall, had dropped into place. Had he been one instant less fleet in his dive through that opening, he would have been ground to pulp beneath it! Strangely, the discovery lifted Wentworth's heart. One peril he had evaded—but more than that! He was on the right trail! Not otherwise would the deadfall have operated in a passage used as much as this one had been so recently. And it meant further that he was right on the heels of his quarry. That this was a way strange to him, that every step was in darkness and undoubtedly full of death traps did not deter the Spider. A fury had possession of him, a fury and a strength that drove him on. Not without thought for the way he must travel, but with a fine frenzy of keen perception, of acutely attuned senses that served the Spider so well in his fiercest battles.

As he darted forward, he dragged a hand, palm-open, along both walls. There was a double purpose in that. He would discover openings on either side, and he would be prepared for any trapdoor which might open beneath him. So he ran for perhaps fifty feet. He felt a turning to the left, a blankness ahead and he whirled, hands still outspread. There was no warning, could be none, of the floor yielding beneath his feet. But to Wentworth's acute senses the first quivering yield of the trap he had sprung flashed a reflex to his hands. No conscious thought at all, just the stiffening of his outspread arms. And he hung suspended while the floor opened to plunge him to some unimaginable abyss. Through frantic seconds, he waited, then he heard the snick of the closing trapdoor, touched it lightly and bounded forward again. His hands still skimmed the wall, but not with any thought of salvation from a second trap. The next would be nothing so obvious as a trapdoor. But he had new reason to hope. The springing of the trapdoor undoubtedly would be registered somewhere. It might deceive the fleeing man into a hope of escape. So Wentworth ran softly. The sound of his passage was a mere echo through the cavern. Abruptly, he paused, listening. The echoes had come back to him....

Gently, Wentworth eased to his knees. He stretched out on his face and inched forward. His hands found what he had guessed. The brink of a chasm. Some particle spun off into space from the pressure of his fingers and he heard it strike once faintly, and then he heard no more.

Swiftly, Wentworth rose and retreated along the corridor. He stopped and drew a deep breath, then whirled and darted back toward the chasm—counting his footsteps carefully.

"Nita!" he shouted. "Nita!"

He raced the counted number of steps, made a scrambling noise with his feet and uttered a despairing shout. He crouched at the edge of the abyss and hurled his voice upward toward the vaulted ceiling and let it die, screaming, fade out as if his body plunged endlessly into space. When he stopped the sound, it was no more than a whisper. Then he lay there, flat on his face, waiting. If he knew Tang-akhmut, the man would not be satisfied with a report of the death of the Spider. He would come to verify it, and when he did... When he did....

The thought of Nita in the hands of the cat-cruel Pharaoh

chilled Wentworth to the heart. But he was helpless in this pursuit through the dark. There might have been, undoubtedly were, a dozen secret doorways opening from the way he had come, and into any one of them Nita might have been carried. His only hope was to obtain a guide through this maze, however involuntary that guide might be. If only Tang-akhmut himself.

A point of light glittered far off ahead. It advanced toward him with utter steadiness, not the movement of a torch in a man's hand at all. Wentworth waited tensely, eyes focused on that point of light. It reached a spot ten feet before him and then began to descend into the depths. That was all. No sound, no trace of human presence, and Wentworth felt desperation rise within him. If they planned to plumb the depths with that light to make certain of his death....

He watched the point closely and saw against it the heavy outline of a wire. It would have to be powerful and strongly secured, that wire, to reach to the depths of this abyss. Otherwise, it would break loose of its own weight. Wentworth's mind busied itself with a rapid calculation of probable weight and tensile strength and he rose to his feet with a frantic pain in his brain. One, two, three paces he retreated, then he bounded forward and flung himself out into space! His arms groped blindly, but with purpose, closed about the heavy electric cable and twisted home. He swayed. Far below, the electric light danced and whipped, struck rock and went out. For a few feet, the cable continued to pay out, then ceased. Wentworth gripped tightly with arms and legs and went upward.

At the point where the cable had begun its descent, he found a pulley on a steel rod that reached outward over the abyss toward its opposite side. Along this he swung a rapid hand over hand course.

Twenty-five feet of that and his feet struck stone softly. A moment of scramble and he was on the floor of another passageway. But had he been discovered? There was no way of telling except to wait and see who came. And that was not the Spider's manner of battle. No other man would have seen the chance he had just taken, nor seeing it have had the courage to carry it through. The Spider's headlong challenge to death had won. He was at least in contact with some device of Tang-akhmut which was operated directly by human hands. The extinguishing of the light proved that it was under observation. But how close was that watch? Had the Spider been detected in his frantic bid for victory?

There would be no hesitancy in the Spider now as there had been none before. He got quietly to his feet and, stooping to run a hand along the rod which had swung the light, he raced along the corridor. He found the rod's end in a recess in the living rock, heard the whine of a concealed electric motor. Coolly, Wentworth felt about until he found a loose bit of rock. With that, he jammed the rod so that it could no longer be withdrawn. The hum of the motor whined high, and the odor of burning insulation came to Wentworth's nostrils. He smiled grimly in the darkness and crouched to wait. In less than a half minute, he detected the crack of an opening door which was utterly part of the rock so far as inspection could discover. He shrank aside from its bar of light and when a cautious head thrust out, his hands reached.

There were moments of dark struggle then, but they were quickly and silently ended. Wentworth crushed the man's larynx with his thumbs, stripped off his clothing and tossed the body into the abyss. Now, if they searched, they would find what they sought a dead man. It would take greater powers of observation than the human eye possessed to distinguish whether the broken thing at the shaft's bottom was Wentworth or another!

It was the work of moments then to free the rod of the rock that bent and jammed it. Swiftly, he stepped through the hidden doorway and examined the clothing he had seized. It was a yellow priest's robe such as the lamas of Isis wore. Wentworth laughed softly to himself, closed the hidden door and threw the lever which locked it, operated the motor to draw the rod and cable into their niche in the wall. There was one exit to the chamber in which he found himself, a ladder that led to a hole in the ceiling. Beyond that, he could not see. But he had his report ready for Tang-akhmut!

Swiftly, he climbed the ladder, found that he was in a narrow passageway which he threaded swiftly. After minutes, it became a gallery which circled the abyss he had so narrowly escaped exploring with his death. The gallery circled, ran apparently above the passageway he had threaded in pursuit of Nita's captor. Wentworth increased his pace to a loping run and burst around a curve into a small lighted chamber.

Another lama turned toward him. "Hurry, the Pharaoh is impatient for thy report, brother, and…" The man's mouth jarred open, hung that way. Wentworth's leap was almost horizontal in the fury of his assault. His hands found the man's throat and together they crashed against the rock wall. Wentworth had reason then to be thankful for the thickness of the walls that were carved out of earth, following faults and crevices in the natural rock.

There was a crunch as the lama's head struck stone. He scarcely quivered as he slumped down beneath Wentworth. Swiftly, the Spider's hands explored his prey for a weapon, but could find only a long, curved knife. He gripped it in his hand a moment helplessly. This slight weapon against the hordes of the Pharaoh! He shook his head. It did not matter. He would not turn back now. He raced on—The Pharaoh was waiting for news. Far be it from the Spider to delay him for a moment!

He twice saw shadowy figures on guard and they sped him on his way with encouraging shouts, with queries about the Spider. Wentworth made no answer. Would a slave of the Pharaoh dare to impart news to others for which the master waited? He passed a fourth guard and saw the man swiftly touch a lever. Ahead of him, a curtain of rock lifted and Wentworth realized that in another moment he would be in the presence of the Pharaoh himself! He touched the hilt of the knife in his sleeve once, then burst into the presence. Instantly, he threw himself on his knees as he had seen others do in the presence. The sonorous voice of Tang-akhmut impatiently bade him rise, advance and speak.

Wentworth sprang to his feet and saw then the circle of men who flanked the throne of Tang-akhmut. But it did not matter.

They could not save him from the one fierce blow that would destroy the Pharaoh and all the evil power he had gathered about him! Pain stabbed at his heart. But what of Nita? Was he to leave her to face the avenging fury of these mad slayers? Must he always face that exact choice between his love and the welfare of his people?

Belatedly, a thought came to him. Was he sure after all that this one man and he alone was responsible for all the crime and terror which the city had faced? Were there not others, underlings perhaps who would rise to take command when Tang-akhmut was destroyed? Issoris was such a one. No, his death alone would not suffice. He must destroy Tang-akhmut, yes, but his death must wait on other expediencies. And this knife at his hand....

Wentworth was almost at the foot of the throne. Lightly he trod the bottom step, vaulted to the side of the Pharaoh's chair itself. His quick action took even Tang-akhmut himself by surprise. Before any man could lift his hand, Wentworth's knife had struck once. The guard on the left hand of the throne fell, gasping out his life, and Wentworth was behind the throne. One arm he bound about the Pharaoh's throat, pinioning him to the throne's back. The other held the knife's point above the pulsing carotid artery. Let him but thrust a half inch into the flesh... And abruptly, Wentworth laughed. He sent the cold and terrible laughter of the Spider as a scourge at the courtiers about the throne of Tang-akhmut!

"Let one man of you move!" he cried, "and the Pharaoh dies!"

And no one moved. No one could doubt the fury and the

determination of this strange priest who defied his master, who held a knife… Somewhere amid the throng a man moaned, and his moan became a hysterical sob.

"The Spider! It is the Spider!"

They knew him then and rigidity crept into all their faces, a rigidity as of death itself, the death that hovered over Tang-akhmut Wentworth's voice rose harshly. "One man shall leave. He shall bring to me the avatar of Sekhmet who this night escaped from the knees of the goddess!" He turned to a Nubian beside the throne. His eyes pierced the man. "Go and bring the woman—and if she be harmed… Go, it is Tang-akhmut's order!"

The Negro fled, his sword clattering to the stone pavement. But the danger was not over. Wentworth's mind was racing swiftly over the course he must follow. Through the passage-way he had come, he must retreat, removing the guards as he departed. Once clear of this warren of death with his prisoner, he could topple the entire structure into perdition. The police might be in the hands of this madman, but the pressure of public opinion would force them to act. A call to a newspaper.…

But he could not permit these men time to think. They might devise some means of attacking him. Heaven knew, there were enough loopholes in his plan. He harangued them in a bitter lashing voice.

"The police are already on the way to destroy this hell hole!" he declared. "Did you think your master had so much power that he could hold a city in subjugation? But others have power, too. Within fifteen minutes, the police and the soldiers of the government will blast this place from end to end with flame. You are doomed, every man of you!"

If he could arouse their terror sufficiently, they would be too occupied with flight to pursue when he and Nita and Tang-akhmut.... His thought died stillborn as across the width of the chamber he saw Nita burst into sight. She fled across the wide concourse on flying feet. Her garb was still the torn, scanty robe of the avatar, her feet bare. There was a glad lift to her face, eagerness in her stride. All the grace, all the beauty of woman-kind was in her rush forward, as if she sprang into the arms of her lover instead of into the path of terror and death!

A stir raced over the assemblage. "The police are already here, Spider!" Nita called clearly. "Their axes are battering at the doors!"

She heard him, then, and swiftly aided him! Wentworth could have laughed anew. He felt, all at once, the strain of the position into which he had deliberately thrown himself; realized that while he held Tang-akhmut physically in thrall, he had been battling, too, against that mighty will. But even the will must die at the death of the heart. Roughly, Wentworth thrust the Pharaoh to his feet.

"Flee, you fools!" Wentworth shouted. "Flee, or taste of death!"

Panic stirred among the assemblage. Wentworth drove his fist to the base of Tang-akhmut's brain and sent him reeling forward, battered to his knees. That half fall did more than all his words to strike terror to those men before him. With despairing shouts, they turned and fled. With a quick word to Nita, Went-

121

worth struck Tang-akhmut again. He flung the man's gaunt, unconscious body across his shoulder and raced for the door by which he had entered. It stood open, its guard fled. Wentworth paused long enough to drop the curtain of stone which closed it, then he hastened on along the dark and narrow passageway. Twice he had to drop the body of Tang-akhmut to fight with the lamas, and once Nita had to strike from behind with the Pharaoh's dagger before the way was cleared.

Tang-akhmut was conscious again and Wentworth sent him staggering ahead of them. Victory was so close now. The men of Tang-akhmut were scattering, the Pharaoh himself was in his hands. He need only persevere for minutes longer, hold his vigilance at peak while they threaded the labyrinth of stone to escape… As he thought the words, the passage came to a blank end without turn or chamber. Tang-akhmut said quietly, "Wait, there is a lever here…."

Wentworth peered into his eyes. "You are very helpful to your enemies, Tang-akhmut!"

The Pharaoh lifted his gaunt shoulders in a shrug, his cat's eyes were sleepy. "When I am defeated, I do not struggle against the inevitable."

"Kismet?" Wentworth jeered.

Tang-akhmut shrugged. "There is a lever. Do you wish to operate it, or shall I?"

Wentworth laughed. He gestured Tang-akhmut to the spot he had indicated as hiding the lever. He gripped his throat with strong fingers, pressed the point of the knife against his right kidney.

"You know what a kidney thrust can do, Tang-akhmut," he said grimly. "Now, pull the lever!"

Tang-akhmut's lean hand reached out without tremor, touched the rock with a peculiar twisting, thrusting motion and revealed a panel. There was a nickel-plated lever within. Tang-akhmut grasped it and wrenched it downward.

Nita's scream cut into Wentworth's heart. With a curse, he drove home with the knife, swung toward Nita. His movements were so nearly simultaneous that he had released his hold on Tang-akhmut before he realized that the knife had not gone home in flesh, but had sliced, then glanced on thick silk padding. Two mechanical arms, like the arms of Sekhmet, had seized Nita and were drawing her toward an embrace with the stone wall. There would be no doubt of her fate, of what those arms would accomplish. Her lovely body would be crushed into shapelessness and dropped lifeless on the floor of the corridor unless....

Out of the tail of his eye, Wentworth saw Tang-akhmut slipping face-down to the floor. He realized that the blade of his knife dripped blood. He had been mistaken, then. He had thrust home... With a glad cry, Wentworth sprang toward Nita, already pressed against the stone wall by those arms. They moved as one, Wentworth already sensed. If only they operated on one pivot there was yet a chance. Swiftly, he seized it. He wedged the knife beneath the highest arm and the stone wall, the tip of steel digging into the rock, the hilt braced against the arm itself. He seized the blade of the knife with his hands and sought to strengthen its steel against bowing, against the snapping which would mean Nita's death!

Through seconds that were eternity, he felt the increasing force of the arms, then as abruptly as they had seized, they relaxed and Nita sagged into Wentworth's arms. She was not unconscious, but a great lassitude, an intolerable weakness gripped her. She clung to Wentworth and he held her close, turned slowly away from the torture rack to which she had been bound—and a great cry rent his throat! There on the floor was a trace of blood, but that was all that remained to show where Tang-akhmut had fallen! He had vanished utterly as if the floor had opened and swallowed him. Staring downward, Wentworth felt terribly sure that this was precisely what had happened. He could see the faint smear of blood break across some sort of aperture.

"Stay here!" he ordered Nita harshly. "If anyone comes, use the lever as it was used against us!"

Nita reeled to the wall, put her hand on the lever and smiled faintly but bravely into his face. "I will, Dick," she whispered. "But, oh my lover, need you go back! There are traps...."

Wentworth's smile held harshness. He stepped deliberately on the trap door through which Tang-akhmut had vanished. And nothing happened! Savagely, Wentworth whirled and studied the wall, the floor on which he stood, glanced toward Nita. His eyes tightened. Tang-akhmut had wrenched the lever down, yet it was up now. That might be due to the fact that the trap in the wall had operated, or it might be....

"Pull the lever down, then thrust it back!" he said.

Nita obeyed. The arms reached out from the wall behind them. Then as she thrust it back, the floor sprang open beneath

Wentworth's feet and he dropped with harsh violence a space of ten feet. Overhead the doors clapped shut again and he was in the utter darkness of… What was that rushing sound? He listened tautly. Water, yes, undoubtedly water, and near at hand. He felt under foot and there was a paving of brick. He groped about and found a railing of metal. Above him, the wall arched and that, too, was brick. Gropingly, Wentworth found the answer. He was on the gallery that ran beside a storm sewer beneath the streets of New York. He sucked in a deep breath and his guess was confirmed. Somewhere in this darkness… His eyes narrowed. There was a telephone system in these sewers for the workmen. If he could find one….

"Nita!" he shouted. "Nita, join me here!"

His voice banged back to him, but there was no answer. Terror smote him sharply, but he reasoned it was only the thickness of the walls which surrounded them. There would be a way back to her. Where he found the telephone he would find a cache of candles for emergency usage. Swiftly, hand on the iron railing of the sewer, he sped along the sewer gallery and finally the blue light that marked the whereabouts of the emergency telephone glowed ahead of him.

The man who answered the phone had a quick intelligence. Within a few moments, Wentworth was through to the one man on the police force whom he felt he could still trust. Lieutenant Jamieson of the detective bureau.

"This is Richard Wentworth," he said calmly. "I am a prisoner in the Temple of Isis, on Riverside Drive. There is a perfect maze of underground passages, some of them natural, some of them cut out of rock, and I am at present in a sewer which is apparently one of the exits. It would be considerable glory for you, Lieutenant Jamieson, to capture me and smash the gang of criminals that is dominating the city at the same time."

From the quick rush of the man's eagerness, Wentworth knew that he had scored. He hung up, sought the candles he knew were hidden at this point and with them hurried back. He could not know how severely Tang-akhmut was wounded. He might perhaps be dead, having fallen through the trapdoor by the operation of mechanism he had already set in motion when struck down. But he vanished from the gallery of the storm sewer... Swiftly, Wentworth canvassed his memory of the thrust of the knife and the more he remembered, the more his doubt grew that he had wounded Tang-akhmut seriously. Silk was a strong armor when padded thickly....

Wentworth had not run entirely blindly on his way through the sewer. He had counted the joints of the railing pipe as he ran so that he knew exactly at what spot he had grasped it; where he had fallen through the trapdoor. Impossible to say how long he had been gone from the spot, but he estimated swiftly that it was not more than half an hour. By the tallow dip he carried, he studied the ground, but there was no trace of blood. Perhaps Tang-akhmut had gone the other way....

Back at the point where he had entered the sewer, Wentworth made a careful study of the overhead bricks, of the floor and the railing. The railing would serve as a ladder for re-entry undoubtedly, but the opening of the ceiling trap... Possibly some such arrangement as that above, a twisting pressure on certain of the bricks to expose a lever. Patiently, Wentworth quartered the surface over his head, trying each brick, and combinations of bricks, and after frantic minutes he was rewarded. There was a rasp and the ceiling swung downward past him. The edge of the trapdoor was recessed into sunken steps. Wentworth set foot in these, swung upward....

"Nita!" he cried. "Quickly, dear, the police will be here any minute, and...."

His head lifted above the surface of the flooring. The hallway where he had left Nita was empty! There was nothing, no one to show where she had vanished... For seconds, Wentworth stood dully staring up the corridor. Far off, he heard the beat of shots, the hollow echo of shouting. A man scuttled into the corridor, the crash of a shot echoed closer and the man, a yellow-robed priest, scrambled on the floor in death. The police were at hand, and Nita....

A groan forced itself from Wentworth's heart. In the garb of a priest, he was foredoomed. As Richard Wentworth, he faced prison and trial for a murder he could not disprove. He had wrecked one stronghold of Tang-akhmut, but the man himself had escaped. And Nita....

There was no help for it. Wentworth dropped to the floor of the sewer gallery and the brick door lifted back into place. Wentworth turned and stumbled away along the sewer gallery in the opposite direction to that in which he had gone before. Perhaps Tang-akhmut, wounded, lay ahead somewhere. But Wentworth knew dully that he did not. Empty victory....

How long he wandered through those galleries Wentworth

never knew. He abandoned his search for Tang-akhmut and began to search for the exit he knew must be somewhere near on the river. He was forced to wade to his armpits in the filthy sewage before he found the blessed sanctuary of freedom. It was night and the coolness of the river as he swam seemed clean to his soul. He grappled the rope of a floating rowboat, managed to get aboard, to climb the piling of a wharf....

It was another hour before he could gather his strength and make his way back toward the Temple of Love. Futile to call in the police, he knew. They would think him mad with his talk of underground temples and goddess of ancient Egypt that breathed out fire! Even if he said simply that Nita had been kidnapped and was held a prisoner there... Good God, he had forgotten that he was a fugitive wanted for murder! But this was no time to falter. He must strike at once, and swiftly. Abruptly, a cold smile touched his lips. There was a way! A fire alarm would send men crashing with axes into the inner sanctuary. All that was necessary was that he produce a smudge.

Wentworth found a taxi and with money that had been left undisturbed in his clothes paid the fare in a northward rush across the city to Riverside Drive, toward the Temple of Love. But when he reached the place, it had an obviously deserted air. There was the litter of moving-men on the walks. He dashed to the door of the temple, forced an entrance... And the emptiness of the building mocked his fondest hopes. Even when he penetrated farther into the maze of passageways, he found no signs of occupancy....

Heavily, Wentworth turned back to the taxi. His eyes had

a grim cast. Under the threat of his escape, Tang-akhmut had abandoned the place, but Wentworth still had a string to his bow. Oscar Dodgington would be back from his "fishing trip"in Maine now. If the Spider paid him a call, the prosecutor would talk! Wentworth left the cab blocks from Dodgington's apartment house, moved ahead on foot. He was a sinister shadow in the darkness from which any man would have fled on sight. It was not that his aspect was so awful, but death stared forth from his eyes; death and the grim determination that nothing should stand in his way! He waited outside the apartment building until he saw the single man on duty take the elevator upward, then he slipped across the foyer and mounted the steps. His reloaded guns were very close to his hands.

He knew Dodgington's apartment. He had never liked the man, but at Kirkpatrick's behest he had visited him several times when working on cases. It was fitted out in the best American-Oriental manner, and Wentworth detested the place almost as much as he disliked the man. At least, he had believed the prosecutor honest, even when he heard Himman's story. Now he did not know. There was no doubt in his mind that Dodgington, if not a crook, was in the power of Tang-akhmut.

IT WOULD be difficult to steal into the Dodgington apartment, Wentworth knew. There would be a policeman on guard at his door as with all prominent city officials… Wentworth spotted the guard from the corner of the stairway he had ascended. The policeman was leaning sleepily against the wall, feet braced apart, head sagging. Wentworth tied a handkerchief mask over his face and was on the policeman before the man spotted the fact that there was some one else in the hall with him. A swift blow floored the policeman noiselessly and Wentworth carried him to the door, punched the bell urgently. He kept doing that until a butler opened the door.

"Help me," Wentworth panted, making a struggle of lifting the policeman. "He's had an attack!"

The butler stooped to assist in carrying the policeman and Wentworth struck once more. It was the work of moments then to tie the two men securely with pieces of their own clothing. He left them wedged helplessly under heavy pieces of living room furniture and moved along the hallway toward the sleeping quarters of the Dodgingtons.

Dodgington was a widower, Wentworth recalled, and his daughter ran the house for him, a girl of twenty-four or five, Wentworth quickly spotted the room where Dodgington slept. His snores were an unfailing lead. Then Wentworth slipped back to the second bedroom and stole into the girl's sleeping quarters. She would have to be tied up before he started to force her father to talk. He bent over her and groped for her mouth with some silken thing he had picked up from the floor to use as a gag. Without warning, the lamp beside the bed clicked on! The girl's blue eyes stared fearlessly up into his, then—her nose crinkled in amusement!

"What in the world were you planning to do with my step-ins?" she demanded.

Wentworth had taken the precaution of closing the door of the room and he had little fear of Dodgington waking. He smiled grimly back at her, still gripping the bit of silk he had picked up.

"Gag you with them," he said quietly.

The girl rolled her head. Her blond hair spilled in golden confusion over the pillow. "What were you going to do after the gagging?"

There was no mistaking the meaning in her heavy-lidded eyes, the lift of her lips. Wentworth cursed. Was the whole nation of womankind bewitched? His eyes narrowed as he went efficiently about the work of gagging and binding Dodgington's daughter. Perhaps that was the purpose of the love cult which Tang-akhmut's false priests promulgated! Surely, immorality was the swiftest weakener of nations, of entire races, and if he struck through the women, a weakened nation would fall into his hands like a ripe fruit! The girl's acquiescence, the slow, languid movements of her body as she actually assisted him with the binding infuriated Wentworth. Only one protest touched her face and that was when he walked away.

His anger went with him as he strode along the hallway toward Dodgington's room. If this damned little lawyer had conspired in a plot which affected his own daughter... Wentworth pushed open the door with no attempt at concealment. A shout rose to his lips and died there. For he was gazing not upon Dodgington, but into the tawny, mocking eyes of Tang-akhmut!

For a moment, Wentworth stared incredulously, then resolutely he pulled his eyes away from those of the man who dubbed himself Pharaoh. He whipped out his gun and in the same movement squeezed the trigger. It seemed to Wentworth that nothing but darkness swirled out of his gun muzzle; the darkness spun and whirled and swooped about him. And now it was no longer darkness, but yards and yards of black silk. It strangled him, settled in suffocating swirls about his head. He went down to the floor, clutching at his throat, trying to fire again and fearing that if he did the black clouds would increase, would strangle him altogether! He flopped fiat on his face, choking, and through the folds on folds of black silk there came to his ears the mocking laughter of Tang-akhmut. Even now, Wentworth could see the Pharaoh's cat-eyes blinking at him lazily, confidently, scornfully.

CHAPTER 11
THE PHARAOH'S COMMAND

IT WAS only when the eyes of the Pharaoh, Tang-akhmut, no longer gazed on him that Wentworth could fight his way up from the black depths. It was madness, this submission. Wentworth knew that his will was equal to the battle with Tang-akhmut. Had he not defeated the man, or at least held him to a standstill, in a half dozen clashes? This was the thought in Wentworth's mind as he surged again to his feet—and found he had been lying on the floor of the hallway; that he had never entered the room of Oscar Dodgington!

Wentworth felt weak; his head whirled. He grasped his gun firmly and checked it over. No, it had not been fired, though he had been convinced in his vision that he had shot at least twice at Tang-akhmut. Frowning, fighting the veils that seemed to muffle his brain, Wentworth pushed resolutely toward Dodgington's room and threw wide the door. Dodgington lay limply in bed, snoring.

It was a puzzling thing, this deep sleep of his. There had been enough noise to wake the dead... Wentworth shook Dodgington, prodded him into wakefulness.

"Get up, fool," Wentworth said contemptuously. "Your time has come! The Spider has come for you!"

Dodgington sat bolt upright in bed and peered into the leveled gun of the Spider. Wentworth had, from time to time, renewed his disguising make-up, and it was the Spider that the cringing district attorney saw before him, rather than Wentworth. And Dodgington squealed. "Don't shoot!" he panted. "In God's name, don't shoot!"

Wentworth leaned toward him, his lips grim. "In what god's name, Dodgington? In the name of Isis, the god of Tangakhmut?"

If Wentworth had expected terror, or surprise, or any other emotion than bewilderment from Dodgington, he was disappointed. Dodgington only stared at him with blinking, stupid eyes from which the sleep had scarcely fled.

"I—I don't understand," he muttered. "Who in hell is Tangakhmut?" Dodgington's natural courage was returning to him. He began to bluster. "You can't get away with things like this! There's a policeman at the door and if I only raise my voice...."
He stopped then, seeing the grim smile on Wentworth's lips. "Good God, have you killed the cop?"

Wentworth shook his head gently. "I haven't killed half the

people you've accused me of killing, Dodgington," he said. "You know that perfectly, but I came to you tonight for a more important reason than a discussion of the Spider's sins. In fact, I want from you the answers to one or two direct questions."

He peered into Dodgington's bulging eyes. "What do you know about Tang-akhmut?"

Dodgington shifted impatiently. "That's the second time you've used that name," he said irritably. "I don't know anything about him. I never heard of him, and furthermore—"

"All right," Wentworth interrupted sharply. "Now then, where were you when you were supposed to be fishing in Maine, precisely a week, after Kirkpatrick was arrested?"

Once more utter bewilderment crossed Dodgington's face. "Good God, Spider, did you wake me up in the night and scare me to death with that damned gun to ask me crazy questions? What am I supposed to answer to that—that I was in Tang-akhmut's boudoir? Or is Tang-akhmut a man?"

It was not the words Dodgington used so much as the tone he employed which convinced Wentworth. Either this man had not been guilty of the things Wentworth suspected, or he had performed them under the influence of hypnotism, so that now he had no memory of them. It was preposterous, of course. There was no earthly reason why Tang-akhmut should have chosen to victimize the Prosecuting Attorney in this way, unless… unless he wished to destroy him!

WENTWORTH TOOK a slow turn back and forth across the room, gestured wearily with his automatic when Dodgington made an attempt to get a gun from the drawer of the table beside the bed.

"I don't pretend to understand all this," Wentworth told him, "but I'll tell you what happened and see if you have an explanation." He told Dodgington then of the attempted kidnapping of Beth Robertson and their seizure when they had gone to the apartment to which Beth's father had fled. And Dodgington's apparent presence there as boss of operations.

Dodgington cursed and insisted the whole story was a lie. When Wentworth convinced him it was the literal truth, a puzzled and hurt look crept into Dodgington's eyes.

"Believe me. Spider," he said plaintively, "I know nothing of all this. I was at the fishing camp in Maine the night you mention. That particular night, I was lost in the woods and didn't get back to the camp until about noon the next day. I finally fell asleep in the woods and that was what made me so late. I know that sounds silly and I have no alibi, no witnesses to support the fact that I was in the woods all those hours."

The very humbleness with which the man made his plea was convincing. Wentworth shook his head. He stripped a sheet from the bed and made ropes of it. Dodgington shivered and protested as he was bound firmly to the bed.

Finally, Wentworth stood over the helpless man and shook his head. "There's an answer to this, Dodgington," he said clearly. "If I find you are guilty, you need expect no mercy."

Dodgington, his big eyes popping above the gag Wentworth had wedged into his mouth, shook his head, blinked his eyes. Wentworth swung impatiently from the room. Dodgington could give him no help, but perhaps Dodgington's daughter could. There must be a reasonable solution of all this mystery. It was clear that she had had some traffic with the Temple of Love and its priests.

Her eyes saluted him eagerly as he stooped over her bed and loosened the gag from her mouth, methodically untied her bonds.

"I knew you'd come back to me," she said happily. "What did you do to father?"

Wentworth untied the girl, dropped down on the side of her bed. His task lay plainly before him. If he made love to this girl, she would talk to him. If he tried to force information from her... He laughed. "I just asked him some questions he couldn't answer. When were you last at the Temple of Love?"

The girl smiled up at him languidly, twisted her young body luxuriously. "Does it matter?" she breathed. "I learned my lessons well!"

Wentworth leaned closer to her, hating himself, dreading the things he must do and say to draw information from her. He wanted only one thing, to learn where he could find and destroy Tang-akhmut. He had determined what he would do if ever he came in sight of the Pharaoh again. He would fire instantly; shoot him down like a mad dog. He could not risk again the battle with Tang-akhmut's will. It was possible that the Pharaoh had drugged him and weakened his will... He cupped the girl's shoulder in his palm, and her smile was brilliant.

"Oh, I hope the Day comes soon," she whispered. *"He* has promised us a Day when only Isis shall rule!"

"A Day," Wentworth murmured.

The girl was ecstatic. "Yes, a Day when all who believe in Isis shall rule. The men shall have free access to all the city's wealth, and nothing can harm them. Though they kill a hundred men, nothing can harm them! And at the end of that day the throne of Pharaoh shall be borne through the streets on the shoulders of the conquered and I shall dance in the train of Isis!"

Wentworth's eyes were narrowed as he interpreted the girl's flamboyancies into cold fact. Tang-akhmut apparently had declared a day on which his looting hordes would have full sway, when they would strike at every center of wealth in the city, a field day of crime! Good God, were such things possible! This modern Hun would loose his looting, slaying hordes upon the richest city in the world!

And at the end of the day, Tang-akhmut would be borne like a conqueror through the streets and in the parade of triumph the priests of Isis would hold sway. And such girls as this would dance in their train. Wentworth knew that the triumphal progress would signalize such license, such nameless crimes as this world had not seen since the looting of medieval cities. But there would be this difference. The women who followed Isis, who had been schooled by the priests of Isis, would welcome the conquering hosts!

THE FORCE of his thoughts had driven Wentworth to his feet and the girl called to him impatiently, her arms lifted. He stared at her with a feeling of horror, then moved slowly toward the bed. It was not the fault of this charming girl. It was the machinations of Tang-akhmut. But when would this awful Day come? How would Tang-akhmut notify his myrmidons?

Wentworth clasped the girl's hands in his, bent close. "Oh, speed this glorious Day!" he whispered. "How I long for the signal to sound?"

The girl laughed. "It will be soon!" she cried. "Will you be there to watch me pay tribute to Isis? How I shall thrill to Tang-akhmut's voice! Even on the radio, his voice seems to reach out and touch you!"

Wentworth gripped her arms, harshly. "Tang-akhmut will give the signal over the radio? When?"

The girl stared at him. "Why, I thought you knew!" she whispered. "Any morning now! The services of the Temple of Love—and then Tang-akhmut will speak and we shall know. The glorious Day! It may be today! It may be that it has already begun! She stretched out her arms and locked them about Wentworth's neck and he heard a footstep in the hall. He wrenched free, sprang to his feet with his gun in hand. In the doorway stood the tubby figure of Oscar Dodgington whom Wentworth had left bound hand and foot.

For a moment the eyes of the two men locked, and Wentworth read in the glare of Dodgington, not anger, but a jealous rage! Jealousy… toward his own daughter! The discovery startled Wentworth. He leveled his gun at the man. "Back to your room," he ordered harshly. Dodgington went…When Wentworth finally reached the streets, dawn was creeping up the eastern sky like white ink sucked into a blue ink blotter. Wentworth scowled in thought. If every minion of the Pharaoh knew the things he had just learned, it was inevitable that the plans should leak out. It must be that Tang-akhmut did not care about that. The police department was helpless against him, misdirected by men obviously in Tang-akhmut's power. Besides, what precaution could be taken that would prevent this wholesale looting? It would take an army corps on guard with bayoneted rifles! For the attack would not be made at any one central point, but over the entire city. The men of Tang-akhmut would hear the signal and immediately such a carnage, a slaughter and looting as this city had never known would begin! A thousand men in a thousand different places would strike. Undoubtedly, Tang-akhmut had organized bands which would take care of certain selected points. Tang-akhmut would still claim the lion's share for himself....

Throughout the Pharaoh's glorious Day, this saturnalia of death and crime would be enacted, and at its end would come the Triumph, the parade of the throne of Pharaoh, and the city's womanhood would dance in the train of Isis! Dance, yes, so they called it, but there were other and uglier names for the things that would happen in the train of Isis!

No, an army corps could not prevent the thing that was just around the corner for the city and the people Wentworth loved, yet one man must stop Tang-akhmut. It was useless to appeal to the State government. In the absence of appeal from the city officials, he could not act. And the officials would not make the request for troops. Any action the Governor would take must follow a long investigation and the removal of the Mayor. There was no time for that. As Clare Dodgington had cried. "Perhaps the glorious Day has already begun!"

There was one thing and only one thing that might avert this disaster. The Spider must find and destroy Tang-akhmut. He must prevent the signal from ever being given!

Sardonic mirth twisted Wentworth's mouth. He, one man, must find Tang-akhmut, penetrate his multitude of defenses and in the end be strong enough to overbear the Pharaoh's will and kill him! And Nita—what of Nita? It was an impossibility, this thing that he must do! Wentworth shook his head. For the Spider, there was, there could be, no such thing as an impossibility! He had succeeded many times before when, for one man, the task of victory seemed as difficult. With such thoughts, Wentworth buoyed his hopes, but he knew how artificial was this courage he snatched for himself.

The Spider was bone-weary. Long hours had passed since, with the help of Issoris, he had made his escape from the Temple of Love, and he had accomplished nothing, nothing. True, he had learned the Pharaoh's plans. But he was alone. Nita, who might have helped him, was the prisoner of Tang-akhmut. Her fate, too, would be decided on this glorious Day, Wentworth somehow knew, and he shuddered to think what fate the Pharaoh would mete out! And Wentworth, even to continue at liberty, must disguise himself!

A sound pulled Wentworth to a dead stop and he whirled, seeking its source, for he recognized it clearly: the chant of the priests of Isis! When he found the source, his cheeks grew gray with frantic fear. The chanting issued from a radio in the doorway of a shop. It was the beginning of the service of Isis! Wentworth's thoughts flew back to Clare Dodgington. The signal for the glorious Day, she had said, would come at the end of the service of Isis! Good God above, within minutes Tang-akhmut would send his men forth to murder and loot! Only one thing could avert that, the death of Tang-akhmut! Even if Wentworth knew where to find him, it was already too late. He could not penetrate his guards in time to prevent the signal, the signal for rapine and slaughter, the signal for Tang-akhmut's glorious Day! WENTWORTH THREW a frantic, questing look about him. The glance had no purpose. It was the instinctive reaction of a man who must find help and that quickly. In a small shop across the street a woman cried out wildly. Wentworth sprang toward the sound. He was tense, every nerve alert, and the action was a release. Through the windows of the shop he caught a glimpse of swift movement, then he was in the doorway. The woman who had cried out was battling against a man who held her helpless. Wentworth deliberately raised a gun and shot the man through the head.

The woman staggered free and leaned panting against a counter. She did not thank Wentworth, she did not speak, only clung to the stability of solid wood and stared down at the dead man on the floor. Wentworth strode out into the street again, the tide of his anger mounting. It was not by such petty bits of action as this that he would defeat Tang-akhmut. He had lost precious seconds. Once more, his glance quested over the street, seeking, seeking for some idea, some slightest hope of help. His eyes caught the inscription across the doorway of a tall office building at the corner, and a cry rose in his throat. Instantly, he was in motion, streaking toward the structure, the Intercoastal Broadcasting Company Building!

An elevator lofted him to the top floor, and a girl behind the reception desk shrank back at a glimpse of his wild eyes. He reached her in a bound.

"Take me to the control room!" he ordered crisply. "It's a matter of more than life and death!"

The girl took a few staggering steps along the hall and Wentworth put a steadying hand under her elbow. "Don't be frightened," he said quietly. "Just hurry!"

The girl began to run, her high heels making machine gun clatter on the hard floor. "Oh, what is it?" she cried. "What is happening?"

"The city is going to be destroyed," Wentworth said grimly, "if I don't have command of the control room within about two minutes!"

The girl gasped and ran more swiftly. At a corner in the hall she pointed rigidly toward a ground glass panel lettered in black. Wentworth flung wide the door. Three men whirled toward him, startled. The walls of the room were covered with Bakelite panels on which switches and electrical meters of various kinds glistened. One of the men wore ear-phones and was turning a dial gently. They stared at Wentworth.

When Wentworth had first dashed into the building, he had in mind only the fact that Tang-akhmut was using a broadcasting station. He had no hope that this would prove to be the place from which the service was going out. He had had a vague idea of tracing the signals, finding from which direction they came, but even that would come too late to accomplish anything. He had only one chance, that this powerful inter-coastal station could drown out the words of Tang-akhmut. Blaring music, released on the same fractional wave-length would serve—anything that was furiously loud. Now, staring at the men, hearing the program that they were broadcasting, Wentworth had a flash of inspiration. The program was a detective story skit, full of noise and shooting.

"I have no time to argue," Wentworth told the control men, forcing his voice to calmness with an effort. "There is a program on the air now coming from some local station. When I give the signal, I want you to drown that program out utterly. You have crowd noise records here, don't you? Good, you use one and turn on the full power of your station."

ONE CONTROL man put down his ear-phones and stepped toward Wentworth angrily. "We'll do nothing of the sort. Why should we?"

"I have no time to argue," Wentworth said clearly. He stepped forward and his fist traveled six inches to the man's jaw.

The fellow went down and out from his pocket, Wentworth drew his cigarette lighter. He pressed its base to the script that lay on the control desk and when he had lifted it, the seal of the Spider glowed there menacingly!

"You will obey!" Wentworth said shortly. "The fate of the city depends on it!"

One of the men held out both hands. "Spider," he whispered.

"By God, if you say so, Spider, we'll smash the station. I'm not one of those what thinks you're a crook."

"Thanks," Wentworth smiled thinly. "Locate that program I mentioned, the Temple of Isis, and tune this station to broadcast on that exact wavelength! You—" Wentworth turned to the second man—"Give me a microphone and attach it so that, at my signal, you can broadcast me on the new wave length. As soon as I finish speaking I want the crowd noise record to go on the air at the greatest volume you can produce."

The men moved swiftly about their tasks and Wentworth stood tensely ready. The current broadcast was cut off while one man made swift adjustments on the giant coils that governed the wave-length. In through the receiving set, Wentworth could hear the final phases of the chant of Isis. By the gods, they would not be a moment too soon, if indeed they were in time. The music died, and a sonorous voice beat on Wentworth's eardrums.

"Our master will speak to you now," the man intoned. "The godhead himself, the Pharaoh, Tang-akhmut…."

"Hurry with that microphone," Wentworth said tensely. "In another few seconds…."

One of the control men hurried toward him with a stand microphone. "When you're ready, sir, just press this button. I'll put the crowd record on and have it ready."

The second man jumped down from the platform beside the coils. "Wave length changed. You're all ready, Spider!"

Through their voices, Wentworth heard the slow and rich voice of Tang-akhmut. "My people," he pronounced, "have implored me to set a day when the full glory of Isis might reign, when the unbelievers shall perish…."

Wentworth pressed the button that opened his circuit. "Monster," he cried, "your time has come to die! The Spider claims vengeance for the people!" He pointed his gun at the ceiling and fired shot after blasting shot. "Did you think," he cried between the shots, "that any one man could defy the people, could escape the Spider? Die, you impostor, die!"

He emptied his gun, waved to the control man to throw on the crowd record and, blasting over the air, all of this whirled into the small control room again over the receiving set. Tangakhmut, of course, had heard none of this. His voice had rolled on, but the words were unintelligible amid the shooting and the shouts. His voice rising in exultation as he proclaimed the glorious Day of Tang-akhmut had seemed to be shrilling in death pain. And now the shouting of the crowd seemed the turmoil that had marked the death of the Pharaoh!

Wentworth shouted blastingly into the mike. "Tang-akhmut is dead! The Spider has killed him! Let his men fly to cover, for the vengeance of the Spider is upon them!"

He closed off the mike then and stood staring blankly before him, listening to the crowd record, to the blending with the program which Tang-akhmut was still putting on the air. It was blotted out, made a part of the confusion. A slow smile touched Wentworth's lips. How long this station could continue to hold the air was a problem. Probably not long. He had gained only a momentary respite for his city, and before the reprieve ran out he must find Tang-akhmut and destroy him.

The control men were beside him, congratulating him. "You beat him that time. Spider," they cried. "You've got him on the run."

WENTWORTH SHOOK his head and explained the situation in terse sentences. "It all depends on how long you can hold the control room and keep this program on the air. Every time Tang-akhmut comes on, you must blot him out. He will hop from wave length to wave length trying to get through as soon as he learns what has happened. What I am trying to do is force him out into the open. If he will only begin this triumphal parade to prove to his people that he is not dead…."

The control men interrupted him. "Get us one man in here and we can hold off all comers. Get the president of the company, Hallwright. He's a good egg and if you can convince him…."

Wentworth raced to the man's office and in cryptic words told what he was doing. Hallwright seized the Spider's hand in congratulation. "As long as I can keep the radio commission off my neck," he promised, "we'll carry on!"

There was no more to be done here. Wentworth had already determined that it was impossible to trace by radio direction finder the situation of the station from which Tang-akhmut broadcast. The signals of the Temple of Isis came from all points of the compass. The only solution was that the service had been spread by telephone wires and rebroadcast at a dozen points. No matter how swiftly men worked, they could find and destroy only a few of those stations and none of them would lead the Spider to the Pharaoh himself!

Yes, Wentworth had hit on the only possibility of victory. If he could force Tang-akhmut into the open, force him to start his triumphal parade as a signal that the Day of Glory was at hand… Good God, suppose Tang-akhmut sent planes over the city with broadcasting magnifiers, the machines that built up the human voice more than a million times and hurled it downward on the earth. He could not be cut off in that way except by military planes.

Wentworth sprang to a telephone booth. He was a hunted man, wanted for murder, but once he had had influence in Washington. He knew the G-men officials intimately. His call went through swiftly and within moments Wentworth was talking personally with the head of the Federal Bureau of Investigation. In terse phrases, Wentworth told him what threatened, what he had done.

"If you will get Army planes over the city," Wentworth went on, "with orders to prevent any broadcast planes from operating, I'll smash the man!"

Wentworth laughed in response to something the chief replied. "Now listen, J. E., you can't get after the Spider until he does something criminal that involves your confounded State lines, like transporting a stolen plane. All right, I take your warning. Now get busy and get those planes in the air." He left the phone booth with the first genuine smile he had worn in weeks. If only the police force of the city operated with the efficiency of the Federals! Why, the Spider walked about the streets in his own identity, minus the cloak, of course, and no officer so much as glanced in his direction….

Wentworth frowned, seeking a way to anticipate Tang-akhmut's next move. The parade… Clare Dodgington had said it would be up Fifth Avenue! If he could prevent that—Wentworth's smile turned grim. There was just one way to prevent it—with the guns of the Spider! It made little difference, so far as detection was concerned, whether he appeared as Wentworth or in the robes of the Spider. A certain stubbornness crept into Wentworth's jaw. It would be the Spider who struck this blow for the people! Let the city that hated and derided him know that once more it was the Spider who stood between them and disaster!

Wentworth crossed the street and entered a men's shop. The proprietor hurried forward washing his hands drily and listened attentively to Wentworth's orders. Once his eyes brushed Wentworth's face, Wentworth had a momentary fear that his scanty disguise had been penetrated, but the man hurried away.

"I have just what you want, sir," he said, "but you will have to wait a few moments. We don't have much call any more for those capes and I'll have to get it from the stock room."

"I'll wait," Wentworth said, "but see to it that you hurry!"

The man bobbed a bow and hurried off. Wentworth crossed to the hat section and rapidly selected a broad-brimmed black felt. He would wear the clothing which everyone associated with the Spider, the swirling black cape and the broad-brimmed hat that shadowed his eyes. Perhaps he was losing valuable time here, but this much he must do for the name of the Spider!

Wentworth drew the black hat down on his forehead, turned to meet the proprietor hurrying toward him with a long black cape of the type worn two decades ago with evening clothes.

It had a lining of pearly satin, yellowed with age. Wentworth eyed it approvingly, paid the man's price and, defiantly, swung it about his shoulders. Now, but for the hunching posture, the limp, he was the Spider. The proprietor shrank back, turned and fled, and at that moment a police car shrieked to a halt in front of the store. Two policemen, drawn guns in their hands, sprang to the pavement and another car jerked up beside it!

Wentworth knew then why the proprietor had fled. He had summoned the police while he had pretended to search for the cape. He had anticipated their arrival and fled from the vengeance of the Spider! A policeman from the second car carried an automatic shotgun with a chopped off barrel. He jerked its muzzle toward Wentworth and began to spew its stream of lead over the shop! They did not mean to take the Spider alive!

CHAPTER 12
THE THRONE OF
TANG-AKHMUT

WENTWORTH CURSED the vanity which had led him to assume the guise of the Spider for his battle with the Pharaoh. It was likely that, because of it, he would not live to make the attempt! With his defending arm removed, who would fight for the city? The G-men could not; the police were apparently in the power of the Pharaoh. Yet Wentworth could not raise his hand against these uniformed men. They but carried out the orders of their superiors. In their eyes, the Spider was a vicious criminal and they treated him as such.

Other cars were screaming to a halt before the shop; squads of police with every conceivable firearm were surrounding the store. And far away, at the other end of the city, Wentworth was sure, Tang-akhmut was assembling his triumphal parade which would plunge the city into a turmoil of crime and slaughter. There would be no one to stop him. If any police, unbidden by their superiors, got in the path of the parade, they would be wiped out. This was Tang-akhmut's day of glory and he would not be turned aside!

Wentworth had a moment's warning of that shotgun attack and it was enough for him to avoid its spray of buckshot death. He sprang behind a clothes case in the middle of the store and the lead peppered its wooden sides but did not reach the Spider. It was well enough for the moment, but already the police were surrounding the store. The clerks were in hiding, the proprietor crouching in some seclusion from the vengeance of the Spider. Wentworth smiled thinly. If only he knew how safe he was from that!

Desperately, his eyes flung about to find some way of escape, of even holding off the attack for a few moments until he could think. God, was there no escape? But there must be. But Tang-akhmut must die. And Nita… Wentworth pulled his automatics and fired over the heads of the police, smashed out the plate glass windows with bullets. They retreated for a moment, then a sub-machine gun began to hose lead into the interior of the shop.

Wentworth caught up a tailor's dummy and tossed it onto the floor at his right. He screamed as the dummy rolled, and a triumphant shout went up from the police. In that moment of pause, Wentworth sprang out from the opposite side of the case and reached the stairs that led to the upper story. There was an angle of wall there that would protect him for a moment, but the stair upward was fully exposed and bullets began to sweep it, to peck at the wall behind which he crouched.

He glanced behind him. A water pipe ran upward and, coiled against it, wheel valve near his hand, was a fire hose! Wentworth's eyes lighted eagerly. He holstered his gun, jerked the hose from its rack and twisted the valve wide open. For a moment, air hissed with the water from the hose, then it swelled full and the stream, two inches thick, blasted out with more than a hundred pounds of pressure behind it!

Wentworth thrust the nozzle of the hose about the corner, and the stream took a policeman armed with a shotgun, in the chest and bowled him over. While the man shouted and the others paused, staring, Wentworth charged with his hose. Its solid stream of water would deflect any bullets that struck it directly and Wentworth held the nozzle chest high. If they thought to shoot at his legs….

THE ENTIRE maneuver depended on speed and the hose dragged heavily on his arms. As he reached the corner of the clothing case, Wentworth wedged the hose in the opening of the door, darted to the opposite side of the case and charged the door, both guns spitting, but the lead flying high. Men shrank back, crouched to each side of the doors. Guns waited for him…

The moment he left that door, he would plunge into a barricade of lead that no living thing could pass. But Wentworth did not crash through the door. At the last instant he swerved aside into the show window. He snatched up a clothes dummy and hurled it at the nearest policeman through the broken window. The dummy swept the jagged edges clean and Wentworth dived through after it.

The police had made one mistake and Wentworth's quick eyes found it. They had jammed in too thickly about the door. If once he landed amid that packed force of men, they would not be able to shoot and he need worry only about their fists, their clubs, their overwhelming numbers.

But even in the instant he was leaping after the dummy, he did not make a false move. He dived after it, but to one side, and bullets caught the dummy in midair, tore it, battered it to a standstill and dropped it rolling to the sidewalk. Wentworth caught a policeman's stomach with his shoulder and rolled him against the legs of his companions. Instantly, Wentworth was on his feet again, darting between the crowded police cars, among the running excited police. Bullets screamed after him but he reached a police coupé on the outer ranks of the thick-banked cars and sprang to the wheel without being hit.

He kicked the engine of the car to life, whirled in a tight U-turn that bumped over the sidewalk, and streaked for the nearest corner. It was fifty feet away and those fifty feet were as many miles to Wentworth. He strained forward over the wheel, jockeying the laboring engine. Behind him, the guns crashed and crashed again. A machine gun stammered into life and he heard the drum of bullets against the metal side of the car.

Almost, Wentworth could see the machine gun's bullet pattern creep up the side of the car. The corner was only feet away now, bare feet, now inches, but he knew, he *knew* he would reach it too late. The speed of forty-five caliber slugs is eight hundred feet a second. Instinctively, he threw up an arm between his head and that machine gun and the arm went numb and slapped him in the head. His arm hit him so viciously that he was hurled sideways in the seat and the car lurched wildly, bumped over the curb. Somehow, Wentworth clung to the steering wheel with his other hand, somehow he straightened the car away from the wall, then away from the lamp pole that jumped into its path. He hurled it, roaring, along the side-street, kicked the siren to its full shrieking violence.

Drunkenly, the car reeled and drunkenly Wentworth swayed behind the wheel. He pulled his heavy head about and stared at his left arm. It had a curiously twisted look and already the sleeve was drenched with blood. Wentworth forced his eyes away from the sight of it. Luckily the bullets had hit the bone. Luckily, or those bullets would have whanged through the soft flesh and found their billets in the Spider's brain!

Dimly he was aware of the sirens behind him, of traffic skittering from his wild, swerving path. The siren of his own car shrieked and shrieked. If he could stop for a few seconds, he might get a tourniquet on that arm and stop the loss of blood. Already, he was beginning to feel that awful hunger for air that came from the suffocation of drained arteries. His mouth sagged open, the breath was sucking in through his nostrils, through his mouth, but his throat wasn't big enough to carry the air he needed....

FIFTH AVENUE. Yes, this was Fifth Avenue. There was the building he had owned, where he had made his home. Where was the parade? Ahead there, was that the parade. He saw a policeman drop to his knee and sight a gun braced against a lamp post. Wentworth watched him curiously, doing nothing but drive the car violently forward at its full, tearing speed. His own harsh breathing drowned out all other sound. He saw the policeman's gun kick, then he was past.

He reached out feebly and knocked open the windshield, and wondered that the car swerved so furiously. This was better, this was better. The whip of the air drove the darkness from his eyes. He could see a little more clearly, a little, not much. The air beat against the roof of his open mouth and still he was panting, he could not get enough air.

Ah, what was that thing that swayed and danced before his eyes there? The parade, at last? Yes, that was it, the parade, and the thing that swayed was the throne of Tang-akhmut. Dimly, Wentworth could make out the great swaying throne chair, but it was not borne by the conquered as Tang-akhmut had planned. It was carried by the yellow-robed priests of Isis! Laughter began to pump at Wentworth's lungs. Breath he could not spare gusted from him in wild laughter. The throne chair of Tang-akhmut and a judgment were about to meet, the juggernaut of justice, the Spider in a police car!

Wentworth's numb foot groped for the accelerator, ground it

more deeply into the floor. The roar of the engine and the shrill shriek of the siren blended in a hellish medley that seemed to Wentworth like the audible expression of his rage. There was no uncertainty in his mind. His intention was very clear. He would plough into these yellow-clad ranks, and when the throne chair toppled, he would pump bullet after bullet into the carcass of the Pharaoh of hell, Tang-akhmut!

The throne chair tottered as men darted from beneath its carrying handles. Some of the priests dropped to their knees and began to shoot with guns they dragged from beneath their robes, but their fire was futile, useless. They were panic-stricken. The priests in front of the chair dropped their charge and fled, but those in the rear could not see, could not guess the destruction that threatened. Some of them stood firm and the throne chair's platform lurched, its front end hit the ground, and up from its seat struggled the figure of the Pharaoh, gowned exquisitely in purple and scarlet, on his head the crown of the two Niles.

Wentworth never swerved. Straight up the ramp that the throne platform had become the car ploughed. It struck the Pharaoh, hurled him backward through the chair. It crushed the chair as if it had been a thing of papier-mâché. Then the platform collapsed under the added weight of the car, crushing the men who still struggled to support it. Their screams rose. Behind Wentworth, he heard dimly the shriek of police car brakes. A frenzy was upon him. Before he was captured… The coupé spilled to the ground with the collapsing platform. It teetered, ran wild, smashed through a gathering rank of yellow-robed priests and sent them shrieking in all directions. Panic was all around Wentworth, sweeping the police with it, overwhelming them in its rush. No single man, no small group of men could fight its way through that streaming river of fright....

But Wentworth was the heart and core of that flight. Men fled from him in all directions. The coupé slowed, rolled gently over the curbing and came to a stop with its nose nudging the building wall. From behind the wheel staggered the Spider!

HIS LEFT arm dangled bloodily at his side and from his fingertips the crimson drops fell. His coat was twisted askew on his shoulders and his hat had long since gone so that his hair streamed over his forehead. His eyes were crazily dilated and his breath came pantingly through his open mouth. Men shrieked and fled from his approach and women screamed and screamed again. But he paid no heed to any of them. His eyes were fixed on a figure in purple and scarlet that dragged itself along the pavement. The gun in the Spider's right hand began to speak. Again and again the lead crashed from its muzzle and at each shot, the thing that wore the robes of a conqueror jerked and quivered. Finally, Wentworth stood over that stricken thing from which the last flicker of life had sped. And Wentworth cried aloud fiercely, torn with rage and despair. For this man was not Tang-akhmut, the Pharaoh! It was his slavish priest, the bald-headed servant named Yetse!

Frantically, Wentworth's eyes peered about him. From a golden chariot, he saw the body of a robed priest fall, saw the half-naked forms of two women leap. They snatched robes from the fallen priests and, with these for clothing, raced toward where Wentworth swayed. The Spider saw them and saw their faces and knew them. Nita and Beth. Yes, Nita… He panted her name. The taste of blood was in his throat.

"I have failed, Nita," he whispered. "I have failed!" He took a fumbling step toward her and his foot could not feel the ground. He looked down curiously and the ground rose up and struck him. Queer that he did not feel that either. He felt nothing. It was night, night already….

He was aware of being lifted and carried, heard Nita's voice beside him.

"Quickly," she gasped. "Quickly Beth, before the police can break through the panic!"

Then he felt nothing.

CHAPTER 13
POWER OF HELL

WENTWORTH WAS fighting for his life in utter darkness. But the blows he struck made no sound. He could hear only one thing, the voice of Nita calling his name. Over and over, her voice rang in his ears, and finally he opened his eyes. The hunger for air that had racked him so long was gone. He peered about him heavily. Beside him, Nita and Beth still wore the robes of the priests. All about him was the sterile white of a doctor's office.

The doctor was looking down at him. "It was very fortunate that you knew your blood types were homogeneous," he told Nita quietly. "Otherwise, I believe that the delay of finding the proper blood type would have been fatal."

Bullets caught the dummy in mid-air, battered it.

From the heavy depths of his weakness, Wentworth saw that Nita's arm was bandaged and he knew that it was her blood which had stopped in him the awful air hunger. There was a gun in her other hand. He spoke faintly. "Stimulants. Give me strong stimulants, doctor."

The doctor stared at him, moved quickly to his head. "I did not know that you were conscious. That is a bad break in your arm. You'll be lucky if you use it again for three months. Two machine gun bullets close together. You're lucky to have an arm!"

"Stimulants, quickly!" Wentworth's voice came out muffled. "I have work to do!"

Nita stared into his eyes and her mouth was gentle. "No Dick, you have done your work."

He rolled his head, forced himself up from the table. His left arm was a dull agony and there was a dizziness that clouded his brain. He fought for words. "Not the Pharaoh," he got out. "It was Yetse in disguise. For God's sake, Nita, *stimulants!* In a little while, it will be too late. Tang-akhmut will gather his men again...."

Nita turned to the doctor; the gun lifted.

"Give him stimulants!"

The doctor shook his head. "If I give him stimulants and he overexerts himself, I can't be responsible."

"The responsibility is his and mine," Nita's voice rose. "Give him stimulants!"

The doctor did as he was bid, his mouth thin and disapproving. Wentworth lay passive for a few moments while the false strength of the injections pumped through his veins.

Even then, he tried twice before he got to his feet and instantly Nita and Beth were at his side.

"Paul Shade has a car at the door," Nita said. "If it hadn't been for him we never would have escaped the police."

Wentworth laughed harshly. He made no other answer. In the car, Nita loaded an automatic for him. "Where do you want to go, Dick?"

"Oscar Dodgington," Wentworth whispered.

Nita gave the order and sat beside Wentworth, her arm around his shoulders. "I don't understand," she said quietly, "Dodgington can't be any more than a tool."

Wentworth's lips moved in a faint smile. "Not even that, Nita," he said, his voice faint. "Dodgington is innocent. It came over me while I lay there on that doctor's table. I remembered…" His voice died. He was remembering the jealousy that had flashed in the eyes of Dodgington as the man had seen Wentworth at the girl's bedside. His conviction of the man's innocence under questioning. The fact that on the day they were seized the supposed Dodgington had not recognized Nita.

They stopped before the apartment house where Dodgington lived, and Shade and Nita helped Wentworth while Beth raced ahead to summon the elevator. They were silent as they moved upward. Wentworth's head felt queer and light. The gun in his right hand was incredibly heavy. They led him to the door of Dodgington's apartment. Wentworth lost no time in ringing bells. He fired two shots into the lock and Shade kicked the door in.

Wentworth staggered down the hall and pivoted into Clare

Dodgington's room. It was in wild disorder, with all the evidence of a hurried packing.

WENTWORTH BROKE into a shambling run. In Dodgington's room they found him, dead by his own hand, it seemed.

The gun was in his hand and on the desk was a letter in Dodgington's unmistakable handwriting.

"I thought I could get away with it, but I was wrong," it said. "The Spider found me out and he is standing beside me now with a gun. He gives me the choice of suicide or execution and it seems to me that suicide is easier. I will go that way. I confess hereby that I was Tang-akhmut."

Nita clung to Wentworth's shoulder and they stared together at the pitiful body on the floor.

"Oh, Dick," she whispered. "He really was Tang-akhmut then, and you have won. But did you make him commit suicide?'

Wentworth laughed shortly. "No, I didn't make him commit suicide. Tang-akhmut did."

"But I don't understand!"

"Just what I said," Wentworth repeated. "On several occasions Tang-akhmut masqueraded as Oscar Dodgington so that if he lost out in the end, he would have a scapegoat, some one who could die in his place. It was Tang-akhmut who was here that night and was jealous when he saw me at Clare's bedside. I was blind or I would have known it then."

Nita looked down at the note again. "But that's Dodgington's handwriting. I'd know it anywhere."

"It's his handwriting all right," Wentworth said bitterly.

Straight up on the throne platform the car plunged; it struck the Pharaoh.

"Tang-akhmut hypnotized him and made him think the Spider stood at his side. He made him write that note, then kill himself."

Beth Robertson shuddered. "But how can such things be," she whispered. "Make a man kill himself!"

Wentworth stared down at the body of Dodgington. He had narrowly escaped suicide himself once at the bidding of Tang-akhmut's will. He could understand. And that man with his marvelous cunning, with his mighty will, was still at large. He had taken with him the daughter of this man he had murdered. No one would ever believe that.

They would think that Dodgington had written the truth, that his daughter had fled from the disgrace.

Wentworth's fists knotted at his sides. He had thought the battle won, and it was lost. As long as Tang-akhmut lived... The telephone rang on the desk beside the suicide note and Nita absently answered it.

She faced Wentworth.

"It's for you, Dick," she whispered to him.

Frowning, Wentworth took the phone and immediately a rich, sonorous voice that he well knew sounded in his ears.

"Greetings, Spider," said Tang-akhmut. "It was a pleasant battle, was it not? By this time, I am sure, you have penetrated the little subterfuge of Dodgington's death.

"If you live out this day, Spider, you will hear from me soon, very soon."

Wentworth said, quietly, "And you will hear from me, Tang-akhmut. The next time we meet, you die! But what makes you think I won't live out this day?"

The deep, musical laughter of the Pharaoh answered him, and the line went dead.

Wentworth set the phone down and stared ahead of him. His jaw tensed.

"The door, Shade," he barked, "go and chain the front door shut with the safety chain."

Nita ran to Wentworth. "What's the matter, dear?" she cried.

He silenced her and Shade's rattling of the safety chain could be heard. Suddenly, he cried out.

"The police, Spider!" he shouted excitedly.

"They say the building is surrounded and you can't possibly escape. They demand that you surrender!"

Wentworth's arm closed about Nita's shoulder's. "That's the matter," he whispered. "Tang-akhmut is near us somewhere. He saw us enter and summoned the police."

His lips shut harshly and somewhere, he thought he heard the jeering laughter of the Egyptian.

"But, Dick," Nita cried, "We are trapped then! There is no escape!"

Wentworth caught up the telephone, got the switchboard of the apartment house. "Did a phone call come through your board for me a few moments ago? Ah, thank you." He hung up and a ghost of a smile touched his lips. "You three will surrender to the police," he said. "They can have no charge against you. Alone, I can escape."

Nita caught his good arm. "How, Dick? How?"

Wentworth said softly, "That telephone call did not come through the switchboard. There is a tap on this line. That means there is a listening post in which Tang-akhmut hid a few moments ago when he made that call.

"I can find it by tracing the wires, but his listening post will be small room. Go now, darling."

Wentworth was frowning intently. A slight smile chased that frown away. "Tell them, Nita, that you were brought here by the villain, Tang-akhmut, and make the others support the story. He hypnotized and killed Dodgington, see, and left you here to support his story that it was the Spider. The story of the suicide note...."

"But, Dick, I don't understand!" Wentworth's good hand gripped her shoulder. "Do you think that Yetse's death alone will destroy this huge organization, or even the smash-up of the parade with Tang-akhmut's followers in it? It will help, yes. It will disorganize him for a while. But while he lives... Darling, here is a definite murder charge we can hang on him. And if my plan succeeds... But, hurry dear. There is no more time!"

For a moment Nita hesitated, then she drew Wentworth's face down to hers, clung to him for a moment.

"Come with me, Beth, Paul. You heard the story the Spider wants. Tell it. We'll delay the police as long as possible, Dick!"

Wentworth nodded, smiled at her and she was gone. For a moment he stood motionless in the hall, then he went swiftly to work. It was obvious the tap had been carefully planned and Wentworth had no doubt that it ended in a hiding place or a secret entrance to the apartment. The swift exchanges of personality which had taken place in this apartment the night he had come to confront Dodgington left no doubt of that.

166

Gun in hand, Wentworth followed the telephone wires rapidly. They led into a closet and Wentworth opened the door softly. Dimly, he caught the echoes of a voice he knew, the sonorous tones of Tang-akhmut! Wentworth's lips drew back in a fierce smile. Tang-akhmut had remained too long at his last minute plotting, too sure of his hiding place. Deliberately, Wentworth lifted his automatic and fired at the sound of the voice. There was a deafening crash in the confined closet. The voice ceased and, with no more warning than that, the back of the closet pivoted and dropped the gaunt body of Tang-akhmut at Wentworth's feet.

Down the hallway, the police shouted excitedly. Nita would not be able to hold them now! Wentworth stared down at Tang-akhmut, peered into his hiding place.

Beyond the tiny closet in which the man had sat was another door and Wentworth's swift calculation showed that it opened into the hallway. Doubtless the door of a porter's closet… He looked down again at Tang-akhmut and stared as the Pharaoh stirred and his cat's eyes opened.

Deliberately, Wentworth raised his automatic and squeezed the trigger, staring down the barrel into those fierce, glittering eyes.

There was no change in them, but the hammer clicked emptily!

A harsh curse strangled Wentworth. He stared helplessly down at the Pharaoh. He was weak and there was no time—and then Wentworth's lips twisted in bitter mirth! Tang-akhmut had doomed himself. To help his hypnotism and deception of Dodg-

167

ington, Tang-akhmut had donned the cape and hat, even the wig of the Spider. Wentworth had intended to leave the man dead, if he could find him in the apartment as he had half guessed he might, with the Spider's cape on his shoulders. But the man had saved Wentworth that trouble, had doomed himself....

Wentworth strangled the curse that rose to his lips.

He waved his hand in an awkward finale to the prostrate Pharaoh, then he staggered into the closet and out its further door.

The police would not search further than that limp body on the floor, but if they did....

The hallway was empty. Silently, Wentworth stole to the stairs, made his heavy way downward. He drew his coat to hide his bandaged arm, but it did not matter. From defeat, he had snatched victory. Without Tang-akhmut, his organization would not reform. *With Nita to press the charge,* police could not ignore it. Dodgington was too important. Wentworth stepped out into the dusk of the day, lying hot upon the streets. He was still a hunted man. And abruptly, he stood motionless, listening. It was impossible, of course, but it seemed to him that faintly, through the dying day, he had heard the faint mockery of Tang-akhmut's laughter....

www.ingramcontent.com/pod-product-compliance
Lightning Source LLC
Chambersburg PA
CBHW020128180626
46810CB00004B/1445